65

The
BEARCAT

by the same authors

Torrie

The Black Symbol

The
BEARCAT

by Annabel *and*
Edgar Johnson

HARPER & BROTHERS
Publishers NEW YORK

To the proprietor of "Dave's Cave"—

DAVID GILLEYLEN

9D

Contents

Part I

The Tipple

1

*A*nother mine car dumped its load
with a crash that shivered the walls of the tin shed, adding dust to the heavy air. Jagged chunks of coal rolled
out in a black river across the picking tables, where two
rows of begrimed men scrabbled through it, hunting out
the rocks and tossing them aside.

Men, they were called, but it was a careless word to
disguise the fact that they were really only kids. Some
of them—the sixteen-year-olds—were shaping out to
man-size before their time; it would soon be hard to
tell their age, young or old. But one was barely shoulder
high to the others, and, beneath the streaks of sweat and
coal dust, his thin face was boyish and strained. The

straight, dark hair was plastered across his forehead; his eyes looked a little unfocused.

Jeff blinked hard to rid his lashes of perspiration. He tried to pay attention to what he was doing, but everything kept blurring together—the endless squeal of the conveyor belt, the noise of the jolting screens that sized the coal, and the heavy constant rumble of it pouring down the long chutes to the railroad cars on the siding below. And the heat. That was like a separate noise, a silent thunder of hot sun beating down on the metal roof. He couldn't breathe. . . .

"Hey, watch out!"

Jeff heard the cry only faintly through the roaring in his ears, and then everything was quiet as he sank down deep into a welcome darkness where there wasn't even a whisper and everything was clean and soft.

When he came to, they had him outside the tipple in the shade. As he stirred wearily, they poured another bucket of water over him. Spluttering a little, Jeff came back against his will. It would have been good to stay in that far-off drift of stillness. Now, he could hear the murmurs of the men.

"Poor little nitwit, didn't have enough sense to knock off a while, just kept on until he passed out."

". . . ain't old enough, ain't fit for a man's work yet."

"He's got to learn. What else is there, for a dummy?"

"But he's just a kid, just a kid."

"Here comes his pa. . . ."

4

Jeff roused at that. Pa? All the way up from down deep in the mine? Struggling to sit up, he held on to the side of the tipple, still dizzy. From inside, the big shudder of the screens came through to him . . . ears starting to ring again . . .

Pa stood looking down, frowning. It was hard to read his face, blackened as it was with grime. Big Stan, the boss of the tipple, was talking to him.

"Your boy's too tarnation young for the picking tables, Harry," he said flatly.

Pa gave Big Stan a look with a cutting edge on it. "Reckon I can say what's what with my own kids."

Jeff saw Big Stan shut his lips angrily. Not that Harry Danver was so hefty, but he was a Welshman and had a name for being tough-fisted in a fight. It was certain that his lickings used to be almighty hard in those days when Jeff was younger. The boy even thought Pa might be angry with him now, for causing all this fuss, but when his father hunkered down on one knee beside him, there was something close and searching in the glass-blue eyes, something almost like pity.

"You all right?" he asked, speaking louder, the way he always did to Jeff, as if the boy were deaf. "Figure you can get home by yourself?"

Jeff nodded.

"Then go. Tell your ma I said so."

They helped him to his feet. His knees still felt wobbly, but he set his teeth and started down the hill toward town. It looked a long way off.

Along the skirts of the mountain slope, the double row of houses strung out in a line beside the little creek that flowed through the gully down there. At the far end of the Row—Company Row, it was called—was the livery stable and McNish's store, the dancehall and the cardhouse. At the near end of town stood the schoolhouse, with the schoolmaster's cabin behind it. Just an isolated little cluster of people whose lives were bounded by the long arms of the mountain that reached down on either side of them. From up here on the hillside, Jeff could see it all—all of it somehow centered around one ugly landmark: the tin shed with its long slanting arm stretching down to the railroad sidings below—the tipple of the Bearcat Mine.

Jeff walked down the hill, feeling a little sick. The mutter of the men kept biting into him like a star drill. Dummy . . . nitwit . . . learn to take it, swallow the black dust and keep on working. Knock off today, but tomorrow come seven o'clock be at the picking tables, put in your ten hours and thank Providence that the whistle blew two times, for work, instead of three, for no-work. With summer getting hotter, less need for coal, there'd be layoffs, and the anxious look coming keener in Ma's eyes every time they had to ask for more credit at the store.

What with five kids to see after, she just never could seem to make Pa's pay stretch to cover everything. Jeff knew he ought to be glad to be bringing home a little to help out. Ought to be proud he *could* go into the mine so young and do a job. But there was no self-

6

respect in it, happening the way it had. Dummy? He still didn't quite understand how it had come about except that he was sure of one thing: It was all the fault of one man. . . .

The heat was making Jeff's head swim again. It frightened him, a little, to see the pattern of black spots start to come in front of his eyes. He'd never felt like folding up in those other summer days when he had played baseball with the gang out under the hottest sun. Something about the close air in the tipple. . . . Unsteadily he looked around for some shade.

The only near patch was under the big tree in the schoolyard. Jeff headed for it, cut across the playground to the pump, where he got some water started and stuck his head under. He let it sluice over him awhile, then turned away, dripping, and lay down under the big cottonwood tree.

Even though school was closed for the summer, it irked Jeff to have had to pick this spot to rest. He had made a stern vow never again to set foot in this yard. For here, in that one-room frame building, the real trap had been sprung on him this year.

Until last fall, Jeff had always taken school in stride—feuded comfortably with the foolish women teachers who had come and gone, season after season; got his knuckles pounded; got kept after school and switched across the rump, which was as it should be. Everybody —all the boys of the gang—neglected their lessons. They'd have thought you were a sissy if you'd ever made anything higher than a C on your report card.

They had particularly admired Jeff; he was so good at misspelling things and making up funny answers. Like the time he was supposed to tell what Bolivia was bordered by and he'd said, "Other countries." So what if he did have to stay after school and write the names of each country twenty times—it was stupid. So stupid it made him laugh. Because he really did know them. Bolivia was stupid. Everything about school was stupid, but he'd been easing along all right until Mr. Thurston came to be the schoolmaster.

Lying on his back now, with his eyes half closed against the sun which was speckling down through the leaves, Jeff thought bitterly about Ben Thurston—he could see him plainly, standing up in front of the room, fixing him with those sharp, clear eyes, brittle as a hawk's. The schoolmaster was actually something like a hawk, Jeff thought sorely—quick and trim and watchful.

He was smart, too. He could trick a person into giving thoughtful answers. Before the whole class, he had gotten Jeff into arguments that had brought no admiration from the gang—they'd even got suspicious that Jeff was some sort of favorite of Thurston's, the teacher concentrated on him so much. Naturally Jeff had to correct such an idea. But the worse he did his lessons, the more intent the schoolmaster got. Thurston didn't believe in punishing people. Finally, in a sort of desperation, Jeff had refused to recite at all; for weeks he hadn't turned in one scrap of homework or put down a single mark on the blackboard. All it got him was a long,

8

uncomfortable lecture after school, with Thurston trying to talk and Jeff refusing even to listen—he'd just hummed and looked off out the window. He thought there had been a minute or two when the teacher had almost got mad—there was at least some satisfaction in remembering that.

Finally the last day had come and grades were handed out. Jeff had enjoyed a brief moment of glory when he was able to show the gang all F's on his card, although privately he'd been somewhat shocked. He'd really expected to make C's and D's as he always had before. (Thurston had been so kind as to explain: "It wouldn't be fair to the other students if I let you pass, Jeff. I'm sorry. . . .")

But the satisfaction of having earned the gang's awe didn't last long. That night, at home, the blow had fallen on him. Not literally—there'd been no licking. Pa had just shaken his head and sighed.

"It's all right, Jeff. Come Monday, I'll take you up to the mine with me. They'll find a spot on the picking tables. And if any of these folks around town talk about you being backward and don't have all your brains, just let me know. I'll bust 'em good."

"You mean—" Jeff had stammered around—"I'm not going to get to go back?" Everybody else in the gang was going back, at least through eighth grade. It was just taken for granted, in spite of their talk about hating school.

"You can't make a sow's ear into a silk purse," Ma had said. A blunt, simple woman, she was nobody to

9

put a thing in gentle words. That "sow's ear" made Jeff squirm inside. Pa hadn't liked it much either.

Turning to Ma with a scowl, he had said, "I never held a hoot for these brain-busters, going to be book-keepers and all that. You got a good boy here!" But the loud way he said it, the rough slap on Jeff's shoulder, were somehow worse than Ma's words. Because it meant that Pa, too, thought he was soft-headed.

Now, switching over onto his belly, Jeff plunged his face into the sweet long grass, hanging onto it hard with his clenched hands. He thought of the black smell of the coal; he thought about the next fifty or sixty years of his life, and the work whistle and the bone-tiredness. He'd always known he would go into the mine some-day, but he hadn't really pictured it to be so hard. It wouldn't have been so soon, either, if Ben Thurston hadn't come along. . . .

And right then and there Jeff hated the schoolmaster more fiercely than anything on earth. He thought, someday I'll get even! I'll get back at him for this!

2

*J*eff's anger was so powerful inside him, he couldn't lie still with it. Scrambling to sit up, he glared at the blank windows staring at him from the deserted schoolhouse. On an impulse, his hand even started toward his hip pocket—and then he remembered. One of the final indignities perpetrated on him by Mr. Schoolmaster Thurston had been the confiscation of his slingshot.

There'd been no justice in it. Out on the playground, that last week of school, six of the boys had been having a little friendly competition, when somebody's shot nipped Aggie Weber on the arm and she'd gone bawling inside to tattle. Jeff knew it couldn't have been his fault—he'd never aimed that wild in his life. But Thurston had taken up every beany in sight. It almost amounted to robbery.

It was the best slingshot Jeff had ever made, too. The cast was long and strong; he'd chosen the wood for the crotch carefully and traded ten of his best aggies for the rubber, which another boy had brought out all the way from Pittsburgh. A really choice piece of rubber, thicker and stretchier than any he had ever owned. It wasn't going to be easy to make another beany as good, and besides, Jeff was used to the pull of it.

For a minute, he sat thinking. Much as he hated the idea of ever again seeing this contemptible man who had caused him so much misfortune, all the same he decided he'd better go ask Thurston for that slingshot.

Not ask. Tell. *Gol-dang-it, Thurston, give me that slingshot this minute!* He rehearsed it silently, trying to get the right emphasis, as he got up and walked around the school building to the back, where a path led through some weeds to the schoolmaster's cabin.

It was a skimpy one-room dwelling; Jeff saw that the door was closed tight, the shades down inside. For a minute he had a sudden anxiety that the teacher might have packed up and left town for the summer. When he knocked, he got no answer for a minute and was about to give it a second try, when he saw one of the shades move slightly, as if someone had looked out through a crack. Then the door was unlocked and set ajar. He heard Thurston say, "Come on in, Jeff."

As he hesitated on the threshold, Jeff noticed that

the cot just inside the door was rumpled and guessed that the teacher had been lying down. It was an odd thought—he could hardly picture Thurston ever getting that human. Meanwhile the schoolmaster had gone to the back of the room and was washing his face at a basin.

"Have a seat," he offered, without turning around.

Squaring away, reminding himself that he was a man grown, practically, with a job and responsibilities and rights, Jeff spoke firmly.

"I came here to pick up my slingshot, Thurston." It came out pretty much as he'd hoped, except that he hadn't been able to bring out the "gol-dang-it."

Drying his face, talking from the depths of the towel, the teacher said, "It's a vulgar mannerism to address people by their last names. If you can't bring yourself to use 'Mister,' I'd prefer that you call me Ben." He folded the towel, hung it over the china pitcher. Then he turned, and Jeff was startled out of whatever he'd been about to say.

The schoolmaster was a sight! He looked as though he'd come off second best in a fight with a grizzly bear. There were cuts on his forehead and jaw, a patch of adhesive tape across the bridge of his nose, and one eye was blackened and swollen. Brutal welts showed below the open collar of his shirt.

Standing there, hands on hips, he surveyed Jeff almost as curiously. "You seem to have been playing in a coal pile."

The boy glanced down at his grimy work clothes,

stiff with sweat and black dust; it encouraged him to talk right up—no need to feel little and pupilish any more.

"I'm working, these days," he said bluffly. "Got a job up at the mine. I won't be back in school next year, so—"

"You're not coming back!" Thurston cut in sharply. "Why on earth?" And then he asked shrewdly, "Was it the poor grades you racked up for yourself? Surely your parents wouldn't make such a decision on the basis of grades alone?"

With what little starch he could muster, Jeff said, "There's a lot more important things than stupid school stuff. Now if I can have my slingshot—" because the stiffening had started to go out of him again.

As if aware of it, Thurston shoved a chair forward. Jeff saw that the knuckles of his hand were cut.

Sinking weakly into the seat, he couldn't help asking. "You been in a fight?"

Thurston brought the other chair from the desk and sat down. "It wasn't much of a fight," he said, "three against one. But what's this about a job? What sort of work do they have at the mine for a boy your age?"

"I'm doing man's work," Jeff told him defensively. "I'm on the picking tables, making good wages."

Thurston eyed him hard out of that battered face. "On the tables you're making a dollar-twenty a day. Do your folks need money that badly?"

"I reckon that's our business," Jeff retorted. Questions —always questions. It was warm in the little room; he

14

was starting to perspire again and yet he felt clammy, too. He thought if he could just get his beany and go . . .

"So now you're playing hooky from work, just as you used to from school?" Thurston suggested it in that way of his that simply forced a person to answer back.

"I am not!" Jeff protested. "It got hot up there—I was working pretty hard so—they—let me off for the afternoon."

All at once the teacher dropped the goading tone. "I thought you looked a little done in," he murmured. "You could probably use a stimulant." Stiffly he got to his feet and went back to the curtained-off alcove that served as kitchen.

Jeff thought for a minute of whisky and wondered whether he could drink it without choking. But, to his disappointment, the teacher just picked up the kettle that was warming at the back of the pot-bellied stove, where he had a small fire banked.

Coming back with a couple of cups of tea, he handed one to Jeff. "Try it. It's surprising how it revives you—"

Hot tea on a hot day was hardly what Jeff would have chosen, but, oddly enough, the warm drink settled the world solid in front of his eyes again. He began to feel better so fast, he could almost enjoy sitting here, contemplating the bandages on Thurston's hand and face and the fact that he needed stimulants too.

"Who beat you up?" he asked curiously.

"I don't know." The teacher started to lean back and winced. "They had kerchiefs tied over their faces."

"Robbers?"

"No, they didn't rob me. Just jumped me as I was walking up in the woods yesterday about dusk. I'm afraid my efforts to defend myself did them no serious injury, so I'll probably never be able to learn their identity."

"But what did they want?"

"They apparently wanted to administer a beating. Two of them pinned my arms while the third went to work most thoroughly with a length of harness chain. You'd have enjoyed it." He grinned suddenly—it made him seem so young and different that it caught Jeff off-guard. Not only was Thurston accepting the fact that they were equals now, and the dislike could be brought right out in the open, but he actually seemed to like it.

"Did you—pass out?" Jeff asked. Secretly he doubted that he could have made a joke after a whipping like that.

"Eventually. The human body has a very sensible way of becoming insensible when it has taken a certain amount of punishment."

For some reason, that explanation made Jeff feel better. He'd been a little worried about himself, wondering if there were something weak and unmanly about him. But there was certainly nothing feeble about this long-shanked, broad-shouldered young man who thought nothing of having passed out.

"Why would anybody want to do a thing like that to you?" Jeff asked.

Thurston shrugged. "I'd say somebody must have a

hatred for teachers in general and me in particular. Wouldn't you agree that it's a reasonable assumption?"

Jeff knew when he was being kidded. And yet there was no real animosity in the teacher's joshing; it was almost friendly. That thought shocked the boy considerably—he certainly didn't want to feel friendly about Thurston.

"Well," he said briskly, "since you'll probably be going away for the summer, if you'll just give me back my slingshot—"

"I'm not going to leave town—not now," Thurston said, with some grimness in his tone that Jeff didn't understand. "But I will concede that you may have good reason to need your weapon one of these days." Getting to his feet, he went over to the desk in the corner—it was as scarred and secondhand as everything else in the room, but the cases full of books on either side of it were well cared for and handsome. Jeff thought that of all the things in the cabin they alone were not Company property.

After rummaging in a drawer, Thurston came back with the slingshot in his hand, hefting it critically. "I've looked this over with some care," he said in his teacherish way, "and it's an excellent job. I assume you made it yourself?"

Suspecting some sort of maneuver to put them on more sociable terms, Jeff nodded, unsmiling. He was already standing at the door, waiting to go. The afternoon was getting late, the last long streamers of sun reaching down to the valley through gaps in the high peaks—the Absarokas—that rose steep behind the flat bench where the mine stood. Nighthawks were out, swooping after insects with a ripping rush of wings. Jeff knew he should have been home a long time ago.

And still the schoolmaster held the slingshot in his hand as he walked with Jeff out onto the step in front of the cabin. Bending down painfully, he picked up a small smooth stone, then straightened and glanced around. On the roof of the school outhouse fifty yards away someone had thrown a tin can.

So quickly that Jeff didn't suspect what he was up to, the schoolmaster seated the stone in the pocket of the slingshot, hardly bothered to take aim, and let fly— a perfect shot that sent the can spinning.

"I've always thought," he remarked, "that the proof of anything lies in its performance." He handed the slingshot to Jeff. "You've got a good shooter there."

3

*J*eff cut across the back yards of the Row, ducking under clotheslines, skirting washtubs, heading on down toward the fifth in the line of houses. They were all exactly alike—built square, painted a uniform mustard color, with brown shingle roofs. These, on this side of the road, were the bigger homes for the large families; each had four downstairs rooms and an attic which could be reached by a ladder. Across on the other side were the smaller houses, three rooms and no opening to the space up under the roof.

Not that the attic was such a choice spot—it was hot and close in the daytime in summer, and in winter, so cold that it sometimes couldn't be slept in. Right now, though, Jeff was grateful to live up there alone. It was one advantage to having all sisters; they shared the extra bedroom below, and he could get away to himself, away from the chatter.

Girls, he reflected, were another source of his present misfortunes. That random guess of Thurston's had set him thinking: It actually wasn't *just* the grades that had got him into this corner, he had to admit. Part of it was females—all the females, practically, that he had ever known. When you have four sisters, you don't ever talk much—you can't. You get a habit of sitting back quiet. When they tease, and all their girl friends tease, the best way he'd found to stay out of trouble was to keep still and act—dumb. Jeff winced as he thought of how often he'd pretended not to understand what they were getting at, what petty little thing they were snickering about. It had even turned into a useful pose to save him other irritations. Ma had quit sending him on womanish errands after he'd "forgot" things often enough. For quite a while now the folks had called him "slow," but it had always been fairly convenient. Right now, late for supper, Jeff had been gearing himself all the way home to put on his blank "innocent" look.

Swallowing hard on this discovery, he wished he could have a little more time to figure this business out, but it was too late—as he crossed his own back yard, he saw Pa's lunch pail already there on the back stoop, so the whole family would know by now that Jeff had collapsed up in the tipple. He saw them watching for him from the back window, heard their voices carrying on.

"There he is now!"

"Thank the Lord!"

"He looks all right."

Jeff heard his father say angrily, "I told him to come straight home here."

And Ma hushed him up. "Leave the boy be, Harry. You know he can't always remember so good."

Jeff shuddered. With sudden impulse he decided to hold his head up, this time, and try to act—just normal.

As he came up the back steps a rush of warm food smell made the hunger jump inside him. It steadied him enough to meet the whole flock as they closed in—Ma and Pa on either side. The twins, as always, kept hopping around, in front and in back and all over the room, until you thought you were seeing a half-dozen identical nine-year-old, bang-haired, snub-nosed imps, instead of only two. Even the baby, only a year old, teetered over to cling to his knee like a wild rosebush. Jeff picked her up—just to get her out of the way, of course.

"Yes'm," he answered his mother, "I feel fine." And to his father, he said, "I lay down under a tree on the way home. Just felt like resting awhile." Just wanted a little peace and quiet, but then you can't say that to your parents.

"How did it feel to faint?" Deborah demanded happily.

"Did it hurt horrible?" Dorinda grinned with open approval.

Why anybody ever thought those two were pretty or sweet— Unless you'd call a couple of blue-eyed bobkittens "sweet"!

Jeff looked down at the baby riding his arm, babbling a little. He hoped she'd grow up more like Becky, who was quiet for a girl. Of them all, she was the only one who hadn't come rushing over to press in close and pry at him about his health. She'd gone right on fixing supper, though she'd given a look that left Jeff in no doubt that she cared, too. A grave, slender girl going on eighteen, she looked almost womanly since she'd taken to putting her hair up in braids.

Now she brought an end to the hubbub—carried the stew over to the table and took off the lid to let forth a torrent of savory aroma that brought them all around.

They sat down and ate with the silent intentness of hungry people who do not waste the taste of food by talking. It was a good thing, Jeff thought, that potatoes and onions didn't cost much. Ma could make the best stew in the world out of a pound of brisket, though he'd never stopped to think about it much until lately, since going to work.

Or maybe it had started a little before that. Something had begun to raise odd questions in his mind these past few months. Maybe it was those infuriating arithmetic problems of Thurston's. Any other teacher just decently told you to say your multiplication tables, but Thurston would ask something like: If a man makes

$2.70 for a ten-hour day at the mine and gets paid in Company scrip, how much buying power does he earn in one hour? That sort of problem made a person want to blow up.

The paper scrip was a form of note which the Company would advance to a miner if he needed some of his pay before the end of the month. It looked something like money, but you could redeem it only at the Company store, and even there it was worth just 80¢ on the dollar. So you got into fractions and long division, and if you did find the answer it didn't make you feel too good. Now that Jeff was actually working, he resented it even more acutely. It was practically indecent to start a person thinking how little his wages could buy.

Thurston had an obnoxious way of teaching history, too. Instead of sticking to Custer's last stand and the rest of the usual Montana history, he made them all memorize a lot of stuff—the Preamble and the first paragraph of the Declaration and the whole of the Gettysburg thing! Not that Jeff had done it. It occurred to him to wonder whether he could have if he'd tried. . . .

Somebody giggled, as if they could read his mind. He ducked his head over his plate. Deb and Dorrie usually quieted down to eat, but tonight they couldn't help giggling whenever they looked at Jeff. And as soon as the meal was over, they rushed out into the back yard, where they could practice collapsing into each other's arms with terrible strangling noises, followed by screams of laughter.

As the rest of the family finished the dessert of corn-

prayer meeting would amount to that much, but that's what he did."

"I told you we was lucky." Ma looked around at them accusingly. "It ain't every town got a Deacon and a prayer meeting of its own every Sunday. Now maybe this back-slid family will join me and go." She'd been trying to get them to meeting ever since the Deacon had chosen this town to come and save, a few months back.

Pa didn't commit himself, one way or the other. Jeff could see he was turning something else over in his mind. Abruptly shoving back from the table, he got up.

"They're not going to scare us, though," he growled, as he stalked off into the living room.

Ma took the dishes to the sink absently. Jeff knew it was hopeless to ask her, but curiosity burned like pepper inside him.

"Who?" he repeated. "Who's 'they'?"

Ma stared at him as if he weren't there. "I think I'll go see Molly Winkler."

Becky was already pouring hot water into the dish-pan. "Go along, Ma, I'll do these." And when she and Jeff were alone, she said it over again, as if he couldn't understand. "I'll do them. You don't need to help."

"Sure, I'll help." He certainly didn't want to, but the way everybody was shucking him off, he just had to take a stand about something.

Becky looked surprised. Ever since Jeff had been go-ing to work, he'd been let off the house chores, as a working man should be. Now she came over and laid a hand on his shoulder, as if to test whether he was solid or not.

"Do you really feel all right?" she asked anxiously.

"Of course I do! I just—it was just hot today."

"And summer only beginning!" All at once, she put an arm around his shoulders and held him tight—a swift little embrace that made Jeff suddenly feel shy. She'd never done such a thing before.

"It's not right," she said, under her breath. Becky seldom spoke out hard, and Jeff had never seen her lose her temper, but now she looked angry, and for his sake too.

"I'll get used to it," he told her awkwardly, wanting to comfort her.

"Yes, I suppose you will," she sighed. "Everybody does. The mine swallows men up."

"It's not going to swallow me up yet," Jeff assured her. "I don't even get to go into the shaft until I've been a picker for a couple of years."

"That's not what I meant." She let him go and turned to wash the dishes.

But then nobody could tell just what Becky meant. She was set apart from the others almost as much as he was, except that nobody had ever accused her of being dumb—she'd made all A's in school, and that was likely her trouble, Jeff thought. It must surely be the reason she never was courted by any fellows, for otherwise she was as well favored as most girls.

28

He wondered, suddenly, if Becky, with all her brains, understood what was going on in this town.

"What kind of trouble was Pa talking about?" he asked. "Do you know?"

She didn't answer right away. Then, in a low voice, she said, "I know one thing. You'll be best off to stay away from Ben Thurston."

4

"Come, come, come, come,
Come to the church in the wildwood. . . ."

Ma's soprano reached out, fair and hearty, over most of the other ladies' voices, and Pa's "come's" sounded like the booming of a bass drum. It startled Jeff to hear his parents swing into the hymn that way, since as far back as he could remember they had never been to a church. Attending prayer meeting was a big concession by his father, who always maintained that the Lord said Sunday was a day of rest and he believed in following instructions.

Now, though, shaved and clean-shirted and with his

hair plastered down, he was making a good stab at being holy. Ma was downright uplifted, and even the twins, stationed between Ma and Becky, were being good. All starched up in their best shirtwaists and pinafores, with red bow-ribbons tied under their chins, they looked proper as a couple of Christmas packages.

With the song over, the Deacon was starting on the final round of prayers. A little man, plump, almost bald, he had a face as pink and smooth as celluloid, the dark eyes seeming almost too large for it. He never closed them when he prayed—just looked up in the general direction of heaven and spoke to someone there as if they were on good terms.

He was going on now about the Lord being everybody's shepherd. Jeff tried not to fidget, but his suspenders seemed a good deal tighter than they had the last time he dressed up in his Sunday clothes. He wondered hopefully if his shoulders were getting broader, maybe putting on some muscle; he tried to steal a glance down at them, but Pa shoved an elbow in his ribs and he came to attention.

This idea of being a sheep didn't really appeal to Jeff, but he supposed you couldn't take it too literally. The Deacon was going on to explain how you'd be led into a pasture when you died, but that seemed a long time away to Jeff. He was more troubled about what happened between now and then.

The Deacon was telling them not to worry about that. The main thing was that you shalt not want a lot of things you can't have, and people should be thankful for what they did have. He said to consider the poor starving aborigines of Armenia and Ethiopia. Then everybody joined him in an extra prayer for the poor Winklers, "cast adrift and wandering, jobless." Finally they finished by singing "From Greenland's icy mountains, from India's coral strand," which made Jeff feel the whole melancholy hungry world stretching off on every side of them. All in all, the prayer meeting hadn't helped him personally very much.

It wasn't until they got up to file out that Jeff saw Ben Thurston. The teacher had been sitting far at the back of the dancehall, where the meeting was always held. Now, as he stood up to walk out with the others, a good many people were noticing him for the first time. Jeff could hear the little buzz start up.

"My lands," Ma whispered, "he really got bashed!"

Actually the schoolmaster looked better than he had a few days before. His black eye was coming back to normal and the cuts were healing. His starched white collar was buttoned up close under his chin and held with a neat string tie. It just about hid the bad purple bruises of the beating.

As everybody milled around at the doorway, he nodded to the kids and spoke politely to the older folk, who hesitated and only answered cautiously. This struck Jeff as peculiar, because they had come to treat him with some respect after this year of school. They even seemed to like him pretty well, for an Easterner. Watching them act so standoffish now, Jeff was reminded of Becky's warning of a few nights ago. Something seemed to be afoot that nobody was willing to talk about.

He was puzzling over it as they lined up outside to shake the Deacon's hand—which seemed the necessary thing to do—when from somewhere came a titter, and a girlish voice rose singsong out of the crowd.

"Duncey-duncey-Dan-ver, flunkey-flunkey-Danver!"

Thin, but it cut through the murmur like a knife. Everybody heard it. Jeff went hot as he glanced to see who had said it. Aggie Weber—you might know! The cattiest little snip in the whole seventh grade. And you can't even sock a girl. He turned his back on her, but he could still feel the focus of everybody's attention.

Pa looked pretty mad, too, and must have shaken the Deacon's soft pink hand a bit too hard, because the little man winced.

"Brother Danver," he said, "it's good to see you and your family here today, but I can feel that there's a worm eating at your soul."

"Oh, I reckon there's a few worms in any community," Pa said, jut-jawed, still sore. "Making a mock out of a kid just because he's slow-witted—"

"Don't cry out against the will of fate, friend. This child"—the Deacon laid a hand on Jeff's head, although Jeff was almost as tall as he was—"this child may not be as bright as most, but the Lord didn't intend us all to be smart."

"That's what I know," Danver said curtly. "It ain't everybody can take up book learning. Plenty good men

33

never was quick at schooling. But I say there's no call to jeer at 'em, either."

"Be not embittered, brother." The Deacon was evidently warming up to a whole new sermon right out here in the yard. "The Devil will take care of the mockers. Take comfort in the fact that the Good Book says: Blessed are the simple-minded, for they will not think all sort of sinful thoughts. Better to be like the meek lambs in the field as long as you got faith!"

By now, Jeff was burning like a coal that's been in the fire an hour—red-hot clear through. Without taking leave, he rushed off, away from Ma and Pa and the whole rest of Bearcat.

Once free of them, he slowed down; he could hear some sort of commotion going on back there, but he didn't even turn. He thought he'd just as soon never look at any one of that crowd again. And yet he was going to have to, day after day, until they quit staring at him and just got used to thinking of him as a . . .

Someone had fallen in step beside him; Jeff knew who it was and didn't want to look up, but he finally had to. Thurston didn't say anything for a while as they walked along, but he wasn't gloating—there wasn't any secret triumph in his face. It was more as though he were thinking very hard, trying to figure something out.

Glancing at Jeff finally, he spoke as if they'd just been having a conversation. "There are all kinds of beatings, of course. The big question is, what you do about them."

It seemed a pretty heartless remark, coming from the man who had brought him to this sorry state. Jeff didn't bother to answer—there wasn't any answer.

And yet Thurston took it as though he had replied. "Certainly you can do something about it," he protested shortly. "Somehow you've let a wrong impression get out of hand. That is, unless— Are they right, Jeff?"

So tormented that he didn't care what the consequences might be, Jeff said between his teeth, "You —dirty—buzzard—leave me alone!"

The schoolmaster looked as though he hadn't even heard. "The Deacon may have been trying to be kind, but he's dead wrong about the Bible setting up stupidity as a virtue. Of course, some people have no real capacity, but I had a notion once that you were pretty bright. And yet, maybe I was mistaken. A really bright kid wouldn't have let me win all those fights we had in class."

"*Let* you win!" Jeff choked.

"Did you think I was losing, those times you wouldn't answer my questions?" Thurston shook his head impatiently. "There have been kids in some of my classes who have had me hanging on the ropes, but not by retreating from me. They used the good old one-two cross punch—they not only took my questions in stride, they threw tougher ones back at me until I was scrambling to keep my feet. I always feel like a fool when a pupil asks me a question I can't answer. No, Jeff, when it comes to sparring, you're an amateur. But I never thought that you were really not able."

They had come to a stop, the boy eying the school-master hard as the words sank in. There were parts of this that he was going to have to think about later. Before he could sort out his feelings, the family caught up with them.

Everybody looked flushed and upset. When Thurston bowed to Ma in that quaint Eastern manner of his, she bobbed her head back at him, but she looked to Pa to do the speaking.

Harry Danver was regarding the schoolmaster with a frown that Thurston met with his own clear, challenging look.

"Good day, sir," he said evenly. "I'm glad for a word with you. I've been wanting to drop by and visit you and your family some evening, but since—recent events—I thought to ask you first if I may come."

Danver didn't answer for a minute. Some of the other miners had paused nearby in the street and they, too, were listening for Pa's reply.

Jeff saw his father glance from the marks of the whipping to the cut knuckles of Thurston's right hand. Slowly, he nodded.

"You're welcome to come. Any time."

Pa wouldn't be pumped about the significance of that taut little encounter with the schoolmaster. All he'd say afterward was, "Thurston's got more stuff in him than I'd have figured. I'm not going to turn away a man like that, though what he wants to come see us for, I don't know and I'm not guessing."

And yet there was no doubt that he was all stirred up—about everything. That afternoon, instead of taking off his shoes and stretching out on the sofa for a nap, as he always did after dinner on Sunday, he suddenly announced it was a good day to make some ice cream. As he went to rummage under the front porch for the freezer, he looked grimmer than sin.

Jeff understood, in a way. It's a suffering shame to have a family you can't be proud of. Not just himself, but Becky, too. There was a big picnic going on up at the reservoir this afternoon. All the young men had invited their best girls. And Pa had been trying all day not to seem to notice that Becky hadn't been bid to it. He seemed to feel worse about it than she did, but then Becky wasn't one to let on whether she cared or not.

So the ice cream was to make it up—to make up everything to everybody. As Jeff turned the crank on the freezer, standing out in the mild sunlight in the back yard, with Ma and the girls fussing around, bringing out chairs and a folding table and napkins, like a picnic of their own, and Pa cracking up more ice—it all seemed peaceful, as though they ought to be happy, like the Deacon said. And yet Jeff thought an uneasiness lay over them and he could hardly say why.

Ma came past, reviewed the way the ice cream turned, and told him, "When it's done, you just lick the paddle yourself, Jeff. Them twins been naughty, they don't get it this time."

That was breaking an old custom, for it was supposed to be the youngest ones who got that special licked-off cream that tasted so much better as it came straight from the cold metal of the dasher. And since the baby wasn't old enough yet, it always fell to the twins, who usually clustered in on all sides of him a half-hour before the ice cream was ready. Now he saw them hanging back beside the lilac bush, looking chastised but not particularly sorrowful.

"What did they do now?" he asked.

"Never mind," his mother said. "They just acted up after meeting today. Seems like they never will straighten out into young ladies." She gave the two a dark look and went back into the house.

After a while, Becky came over to his side. "Do you want me to take a turn at that?"

Jeff shook his head. But he couldn't help thinking that it was nice of her to offer. In fact, Becky was growing up into a very nice girl, as girls go. If a man were going to get bogged down with a wife, she wouldn't be the worst. So why didn't any of the fellows come around? He was turning the question over in his mind when somebody whistled out in the side yard.

"Hey, there, where is everybody?" And Sammy Yates rounded the corner of the house.

He was still duded up in his meeting clothes—a big good-looking fellow with curly blond hair and shoulders like a boxcar. His hands looked like hardrock, too. In fact, if Jeff had been a wishing sort, he'd have wished that he would fill out to look exactly like Sammy. Besides, he was stable boss of the mine, and young for the job at that. Everybody said he was a real go-getter. Jeff didn't know about that, but he did envy Sammy, working with those horses all day. Right now, of course, he looked fairly awful—flannel pants and a round straw hat tucked under his arm, as stiff as a painted picture.

"Afternoon," he said politely to Ma. "I saw you all in meeting this morning, just got the idea I ought to drop over. Seems like a month of Sundays since I said howdy." He was looking at Becky as he spoke.

"Well—howdy, Sammy." She smiled a little.

Ma was blinking, pleased as pie. "Sammy Yates, I reckon we ain't seen you since you and Becky was in grade school!" Which wasn't exactly true, inasmuch as he passed their house every day on the way to the mine and back.

"Well, I been workin' pretty hard, tryin' to get ahead," Sammy said piously.

"Hear you've done real fine, too." Ma beamed. "Good thing for a young fellow to be ambitious."

"Oh, I'm going on up as far as I can get," Sammy told them. "But that don't mean I got to be lonesome whiles I got time free, does it? I mean when I saw Becky this morning at meeting, why I just suddenly thought how I just ain't had no social life a-tall lately. By gee, I hardly didn't recognize her, either. She was so smart in school, I never figured she'd grow up so pretty."

"Oh, she wasn't so smart as all that," Ma hastened to apologize.

"Don't get me wrong—I wouldn't hold it against a person." Sammy grinned generously.

It was all very sociable. As they chatted and laughed, Jeff turned the crank on the freezer unhappily. At least, for Becky the day was turning out all right.

When the ice cream was ready, Ma took the canister to the table while Jeff lugged off the tub of salt water and melting ice. Following him around the side of the house a minute later came the twins, Deborah obediently carrying the dasher at arm's length while Dorinda stared at it hungrily. Without a word, they gave it to him. And stood.

Jeff knew, and knew that they knew, that he couldn't enjoy licking that paddle so long as they watched like that. He handed it back.

"Go ahead, have it."

And as they went to it, squabbling just kindly with each other over who was to get first lick, he said curiously, "What sort of mess did you get into this morning, made Ma so riled?"

Deborah was licking, but Dorinda took time to smile at him in that innocent way women have.

"We just punched Aggie Weber's nose," she said.

And Deb mumbled, "I kicked her shins, too."

Jeff stared at them aghast. That would really relay the incident around the listening ears of Bearcat. Dryly he said, "Thanks," and left, before the urge to throttle them got any stronger.

As he went to join the others in the back yard, the clock must have touched four, because the whistle on the boilerhouse let off its first wheeze—a hoarse, uneven croak that rose gradually to a full-throated shriek. Jeff stopped short, waiting. The people gathered around the table broke off their conversation. All over town, a stillness fell as the whistle let off its second blast. And then, when the echoes had died out across the foothills and the silence was stretched to the breaking point, it cut loose again with a third strident screech.

No work tomorrow. It was written in the long faces of the men and the tight little frowns of the women. Jeff tried to look disgusted, too, but actually he was swarmed over by desperate relief. It was as if, somehow, tomorrow was the most important day in the world and he had nearly lost it.

5

*T*hat next morning—that brittle bright summer morning—was like a thousand other beautiful days that had been squandered in other summers. As Jeff mounted the embankment to the railroad tracks, he was thinking of all those easy weeks that used to drift away. Now, to use these few choice hours of freedom just right, to taste every minute of them, gave him a new awareness.

The tracks were inviting. Stretching away down the valley, the steel rails beckoned on and on, to some unknown place where the Montana, Wyoming & Southern joined another bigger railroad, the Northern Pacific, and from there the way led out of this tight little world, far off to the ends of the country.

Jeff walked a rail all the way to Scotch Coulee without one misstep, just to prove to himself that he hadn't lost his old knack. There, almost reluctantly, he left the tracks and cut on up through the little mine camp. Scattered along a steep dry gulch, it was a scrabble of shacks and tarpaper huts—a few bigger houses that rambled in all directions as if the rooms had been added on one at a time as a family grew.

Nobody knew why the camp was called Scotch Coulee. There certainly weren't any Scotch people living there. It was rare even to hear a word of English spoken, for the populace was mostly Italian, Polish, Montenegrin—all sorts of different gabble rose from the yards.

Jeff supposed they could understand each other, though. They always seemed to be laughing, having some sort of holy day celebration, with queer, lusty dancing and singing. He'd always envied them before —even envied their different houses, each one whacked together just to a man's own liking. But he wasn't jealous any more.

Now that he was working at the mine, he saw that these men were always given the dirtiest jobs, sometimes dangerous work. Though they were mostly muckers and loaders, they were the ones sent to search out gas seepage down deep in the darkness of the new entries, where even the flicker of a carbide lamp could touch off an explosion.

They were lowest paid, too. He was beginning to understand why, in the summertime, there were always

43

so many girls in old-country dresses sprinkled over the hillsides above the coulee. For all that they chattered and seemed gay enough, it wasn't flowers they were picking, but dandelion greens, lambs'-quarters, mushrooms, berries—searching out the meager bounty of the rocky slopes just to have a little more to eat.

Pa called them "dumb furriners" and said they were too stupid to know when they were being poorly used, but Jeff couldn't help wondering. How do you ever protest against anything if you can't speak the language of the bosses? Or even if you can speak it?

Up beyond the coulee, the land leveled off into a flat grassy meadow, with the reservoir just beyond, and there, already ahead of him, the gang was collecting at the near end of the baseball field. On the far side, the Scotch Coulee team was grouping. When Jeff saw the fellows, he felt better. He'd had this rankling anxiety that, for some reason, they might have decided not to come up here today.

The bunch looked surprised to see Jeff, grinned uncertainly, and made a few offhand gestures of welcome. For a minute, things were fairly awkward.

"Hey, boy, how's everything?"

"Whatcha doin', takin' off work?"

"Naaa, don't you know it's no work today?"

They fooled around, punching each other aimlessly.

"How's the team doing these days?" Jeff asked. "You got a good catcher this year?" Because last summer that had been his spot—best catcher they'd ever had, could

44

peg a ball to second like a shot, never missed a foul tip. . . .

"Yeah, Freck's doin' real good," Bo told him—Bo was captain and leader of the gang.

There was a moment of strangeness and then Bo asked slowly, "Did you want to play today?"

"Oh—" Jeff shrugged as if the thought hadn't occurred to him. "I don't know, I'm kind of out of practice." He was thinking that a catcher really has to be in shape, it's no come-lately kind of job. He couldn't blame them for probably wanting to stick with Freck.

"Listen, we could put you in the outfield," Bo said. "We only got Peewee and he's pretty little."

Peewee, ten years old and all elbows, grinned weakly but his eyes showed hurt. Somehow, Jeff just couldn't take away a rookie's chances.

"Naaa," he said nonchalantly. "I don't want to play. Besides, Peewee needs the experience."

They looked relieved. They could even loosen up and ask how it was at the mine, did he like it, and all that.

Jeff answered stoutly. Sure. Everything was just hunky-dory. No, it wasn't tough. Just—well, you put in a day's work.

"I wisht my ma would let me quit school and go to work," said Gordie Smith sadly. Gordie was really slow —he was thirteen and still in the fifth grade, and that was no joke. Jeff didn't feel any particular comfort in being envied by Gordie.

45

Bo shook his head. "Not for me. Work is a pain in the neck. I'll be workin' the rest of my life. Right now, I'll mess around and put up with school a while longer. I may even go on to high."

Irritably, Jeff thought this was a fine time to start talking like that, after they'd all sworn to hate school unto the death.

"Me, too," Freck was saying. "I'm not in no hurry to go down that shaft. Last winter it was so dirty cold, my pop got the rheumatiz to where he was near crippled. One of those entries he was in had water up to your knees. Pop says he's not gonna take it another winter, workin' straight through Sundays and all."

The same kind of disquiet came over them that seemed to seize hold of the grownups whenever somebody made talk like that. Bo laughed uneasily. "He'll take it. What else?"

"What else? Maybe something's gonna get done about it, that's what else," snapped Freck, turning to Jeff for support. "Go on, tell these guys I'm not kidding."

He seemed to think Jeff ought to know what he was hinting at. Falling back on his father's favorite remark, Jeff said, "I don't know and I'm not guessing."

"Sure," Bo said scornfully, "it's not safe to talk, don't you know that, Freck, you dumb bunny?"

"Not safe? Here?" Freck tried to laugh it off. "Don't scare me."

"You can't tell," Peewee put in, his eyes big in his

46

freckled face. "My old man says there's stool pigeons everywhere—there's gotta be, or Regan wouldn't know so much about all that goes on down in the shaft."

They looked to Jeff again.

He frowned, fiddled with his slingshot in judicial silence, wishing acutely that he didn't have quite such a close-mouthed father. A person really ought to know what's going on. . . .

"Besides," Peewee piped up again, "look at what happened to Mr. Thurston."

Jeff glanced over sharply at that. Here it was again, this peculiar way of connecting the schoolmaster with the mine, and a ten-year-old child seemed to know more about it than he did.

Bo was grinning. "Yeah, that must have been a humdinger. I wisht I'd been there to watch. I heard there was ten men with clubs, they knocked all his teeth out."

"No, they just socked him a couple of times," Freck contradicted with authority.

And to Jeff's relief, Gordie asked the question for him. "What's teacher got to do with the mine?"

"Don't you know? He got a secret warning, to get out of town and stay out. So he wouldn't do it."

This was news to Jeff. Cautiously, he said, "I still don't see what harm he could do."

"He asks too many questions," Bo said ominously.

And Freck added, "Don't you know how he's always dropping in? He comes over to see why you missed school or something and then he sits there with your

47

folks and they gab along. Last time he came to our house, my pop got so worked up he was ready to explode."

"Why?" Jeff asked skeptically.

"Well, they got to talking about how Regan runs the mine. I didn't hear it all—they always send you on out—but Thurston was asking questions, and you know how he can provoke you."

Which was true enough, Jeff thought. It was beginning to make more sense. Nobody lasted long around Bearcat if they asked questions about the way Pete Regan ran the mine. But Jeff still couldn't imagine why the schoolmaster should mix into that. He was about to sound them out a little further when the Scotch Coulee team advanced across the field. The bunch broke off their talk, then—bristled up, glowering, slashing the air with the bat, stomping around home plate. Jeff himself had had a particularly mean way of slamming the ball into his mitt. Right now, it seemed kiddish and unimportant.

He drifted over to one side, then a little farther until finally, unnoticed, he reached the edge of the woods above the field.

For a minute he lingered, watching them, feeling empty inside. Then turning his back on the whole ungrateful lot, he headed up into the mountains—the steepest climb he could pick.

High up on top of old Rollyrock, the wind blows all the time, from some place deep in the limitless stretches of sky. Fitfully it burst against Jeff, who sat braced on the brow of the summit; a few inches from his feet the rimrock fell away a thousand feet straight down. To get here at all, he'd had to take a long, tough trail that brought him up to the top of the mountain by laborious switchbacks.

Now it was deep into the afternoon and he hadn't had anything to eat. He was going to be late for supper, too, but he didn't care. For a few minutes, he was on top.

Nobody could look down on him except the eagle up there, leaning against the breeze with its powerful wings; suddenly it tilted and slid off downwind . . . five . . . ten miles, without a stroke, until it was only a dot far out over the face of the Absarokas. And Jeff was alone.

He knew he ought to be thinking. There was plenty to be figured and—what had Thurston said?—what to do about it? But he didn't want to think, he just wanted to sit here numbly. He wished he could stay up here by himself forever.

From here, Bearcat looked like a toy town, and the mine, only some small scrap tin—a handful of junk discarded in a pocket of the mountain. Beyond the foothills, the land dropped off and the country flattened out into plains—cattle land—clear off to the horizon as far north and east as he could see. Billings was out there somewhere. To the south, the earth wrinkled up again, dry and eroded, then steepened into timber country—the Bighorn Mountains. There were still glittering crests of snow on those peaks. And somewhere beyond were Denver, Kansas City, just names that Jeff couldn't fit to any picture in his mind. Big places where you could go and be somebody. People would treat you like a—a person. And if you got to be friends with a couple of other men, they wouldn't toss you aside like a bent fishhook, either.

Moodily Jeff chewed his lip and thought he just might go. Walk. Or hop a freight. And then he had to laugh inside, in the tight place where everything was bottled up. Because the only place he was going to go —he made himself face it miserably—was right back . . . down . . . to . . . the Bearcat.

It was full dark by the time he got down, but Jeff knew his way well. A short cut just above the mine would take him into town the quickest way. He slipped between the bars of the big pasture where the work-horses were let out to graze. He could see the massive animals up on the brow of the bench, black silhouettes against a star-strung sky.

Making his way across the open field, he ducked out of the corral on the far side and came onto a narrow path that used to lead up to the Old Mine, which had been closed and sealed ever since the big explosion a few years back.

Following the trail on down, he skirted the rear of Pete Regan's big house. It always made Jeff wonder, to pass there, what it must be like inside. All brick, with white shutters and a lawn as big as a baseball field, it was a place of mystery. For all that the miners did Regan's yard work for him, no one from the Row had ever been allowed in the house. But talk had got around that it had the fanciest privy in the whole state of Montana. The fact that it was located inside the house somewhere was amazing enough, but there was a rumor that it pumped water and emptied at a pull from a chain. Probably all a big lie. But Jeff never went by without lingering to peer in over the back fence and wonder.

The lights were on in there now and the shades halfway up. As he hesitated curiously, he saw a woman in the kitchen, Pete's housekeeper. She was a mysterious figure, too; nobody knew her. The manager always had his groceries delivered, so his housekeeper never had to leave the grounds. Probably never had time. Right now she was still scrubbing up, cleaning the big stove. It was the handsomest Jeff had ever seen—blue enamel with shiny trim.

And then, as he was about to start on, he saw other people coming into the kitchen. With the shades partway down, he couldn't see their faces, though he knew that one of them was Regan. The mine boss walked with a stride you could pick out a mile away, ponderous, swinging his shoulders like a prime red bull. His heavy bulk seemed to loom in the kitchen, blocking out a view of the other men with him.

Jeff hesitated, curious. There was another rumor around town—that Regan never took off the sleek black Stetson he wore, not even in his own home. It would be interesting to settle the matter and be able to speak of it with authority. . . . And then Jeff ducked—the back door was opening. Regan came out onto the stoop carrying a lantern, flooding the back yard with light. Crouched in the shadows, Jeff was disappointed to see that the mine boss's hat was off, after all, revealing a stout crop of wickerish white hair bristling above the heavy-jowled face.

Glancing up and down the darkness, Regan said in that thick, scornful way of his, "There's nobody out here. Don't be lily-livered. Who would be hanging around this time of night? Now go on and get."

Cautiously a second man stepped onto the rear stoop. The light flashed across his face and Jeff recognized him! Without a moment's delay, he scuttled down the length of the fence, then straightened up and hurried along the path toward town. The words of the kids were dinning in his ears: a stool pigeon, planted to blab on the men, get them fired. . . .

Behind him footsteps were following. Longer legs than his were swinging along that path. Rather than be caught in the act of running, Jeff slowed down, holding his breath.

A hand came down on his shoulder. "Well, there, what's your hurry?" He was slung around and forced to face Sammy Yates under the dim brilliance of the stars.

"Oh. Hullo, Sammy," he said, trying to sound surprised. "What are you doing out here?"

"Question is, what are you doing?" Sammy asked it

easily enough, but his hand still clamped Jeff's shoulder like a grappling hook.

"Me? I'm just trying to get home before Pa takes his belt off." Jeff laughed nervously. "Gosh, I'm an hour late for supper now. Let go, I got to hurry."

There was a minute of silence, then the harsh fingers loosened. "All right, noodlehead, get going," Sammy told him.

And Jeff did.

6

Jeff saw the skinny, blackened arms snaking out across the moving coal, saw two grimy hands with broken fingernails claw at the chunks of rock, seize on them and flip them, but somewhere he had lost track of the fact that these were his own arms and hands. All he was able to feel was the ache in the middle of his spine—it was as if his back had cracked in two pieces and was only being held together by the straps of his overalls.

He had to stop thinking about the water barrel. He'd taken three trips to it in the past—how long? Hour? Half-hour? Anyhow, the last time, Big Stan had given him a look that meant: If you can't stick with the table we'll have to hire somebody who can earn a day's pay. Not being unkind about it, but that was what he was here for, to see that a man worked.

It would be the last straw, Jeff thought dimly—to get fired. Not even to belong to this lowly crew of coal-dust eaters here in the tipple—that would really put him on the bottom of the barrel. A complete failure at everything. He lunged for another piece of coal, then realized that the conveyor belt had stopped moving.

The other fellows were grinning. "Didn't you hear the quittin' whistle, bub?"

And one tapped his finger against his head.

Wearily Jeff stumbled over to pick up his limp, stained shirt and his lunch pail and followed the others on down to the timekeeper's shack, just ten-and-a-half hours after he had trudged up this hill.

As he waited in the line that shuffled past the time-keeper's table, Jeff stared hopelessly at the big black-board over on the wall, with the words written large in chalk:

WORK TOMORROW

Once past the office, the men strung out in little groups of three and four, heading for the washhouse. Jeff walked apart—he always scuffed along with his head down as if he were too preoccupied to notice that none of the men would take up with him. It probably just added to the impression that he was odd, but he couldn't help it—it was a bitter thing, to be old enough to work, but not old enough for man-talk.

And yet in the washhouse he had to mingle with them. It was just one big room with banks of lockers on either side. Half hiding behind the metal door of his own locker, Jeff stripped off his dirty clothes. The water was already on, showering down from the double row of pipes hung overhead along the center of the building into a trough in the concrete floor. Hot from the boilerhouse, the spray was making a muggy mist of steam in the room. Jeff thought longingly of a cold dip in the reservoir, but hot water takes off the grime better.

Advancing into the ranks of wet, naked men, Jeff felt self-conscious, as he always did. Up in the tipple, the bib of the overalls helped cover the baldness of his chest, but here, exposed from head to toe, he felt as conspicuous as a peeled pear in a bushel of pine cones.

As he began to soap off the dirt, he couldn't help hearing what the nearest bunch of men were talking about.

"Yeah, the air got so bad down there," one was saying, "I was spittin' pure coal dust."

Another one laughed sourly. "When I come up the shaft this afternoon into that fresh air, it seemed so thin I dern near felt skimped on it—it ain't fillin' like that strong air below."

"Where was you workin'?" asked a third. "That new Number Seventeen entry?"

"Yep. We're a hundred feet and they ain't bothered to put in no ventilation yet."

And the first added grimly, "I reckon the Company figures it's cheaper to bury a few of us than to give us something to breathe in there."

At that point, one of the men noticed Jeff and nudged the others. "Little pitchers got big ears."

It was one of those silly remarks that Jeff had hated all his life, smug grown-up sneers that everybody thinks are way over your head.

Another one pretended to be surprised to see Jeff. "Hey, where did the cub come from? His daddy bring him to the washhouse to play?"

Jeff started to dummy up, as he'd always done in the past, when suddenly something inside him broke loose and ran wild.

"I reckon if I'm old enough to work for a living, I'm old enough to take a shower without a lot of smart talk," he retorted furiously.

"Well, listen at that!"

"Watch out, Lewk, the sprout's gonna take you on."

"Gonna take all three of us on at once. My, I'm scared!"

"Aw, leave off the kid," said Big Stan, who'd heard the pestering and moved over to the group. "Don't you know that's Danver's boy. He ain't bright."

"Maybe I'm brighter than you think," Jeff raged recklessly, his voice shrill with resentment. "Maybe you figure I'm dumb because I keep quiet, but you might wish you all didn't talk so much one of these days! Maybe I know a few things going on around here that you'd give your eyeteeth to know!"

The amusement went out of their faces like a burned-out lantern. They stood glistening wet under the coursing shower, awkward, incongruous figures struck silent and ill at ease.

Big Stan moved in close to Jeff, seeming twice as big without his clothes—a hulking swart-skinned mass of hard muscle and black hair.

"Now what did you mean?" he asked softly, his voice hardly audible above the hiss of the showers.

Jeff realized that half the washhouse had gone quiet, must have heard his foolish boast. "I didn't mean anything," he muttered, flushing furiously. "I just wish they'd leave me alone."

Stan nodded. "They'll leave you be, and you'll keep on bein' quiet, like you was just hollerin' about so loud. For your own sake, I hope you're not too dumb to understand that."

Jeff went off to dry himself, aware of the disquieted looks that followed him. If he'd wanted them to start having respect for his wit, he'd done just dandy, he thought sarcastically. And picked a good time to do it —a real good time! Because it dawned on him, as he cooled down and looked back at the dripping bunch of men, that among the dark heads showing through the steam haze there was a lighter one just across under the opposite bank of showers—the curly blond crop of Sammy Yates.

Dressed in his cleaner clothes, Jeff didn't dawdle around the washhouse. Managing to get out well ahead of the other men, he walked on down toward the Row alone. It was staying daylight late these June days— windows were just beginning to show yellow lamp-light, checkering the thin dusk. The cool and quiet of the lonesome hour steadied Jeff a little.

And then he came unfirm again as he detected the sound of someone coming along behind, hurrying as if to catch up. His first thought was of his father; Jeff hadn't seen him in the washhouse and had hoped that, since Pa was working on the lowest level, he might have come up late and missed that little scene. As the steps came on, he risked an anxious look over his shoulder—and really did get a start. It was Sammy, back there, not exactly rushing but walking fast enough to overtake Jeff before he could reach home.

He had to take good hold of himself and check a panicky impulse to run. Sharply he told himself not to act like a scared rabbit, or Sammy would get twice as suspicious. Besides, even if Yates had the worst possible intentions, he'd hardly try any meanness right out here in plain view of the Row. He'd be more likely to wait for Jeff to step outside some dark night and—what? What would Sammy do?

And on the current of that thought came another, bolder idea. Up to now, Jeff hadn't mentioned to anybody that Yates was probably a Company spy. He'd been turning it over in his mind, knowing pretty well that nobody would listen to the chatter of a lamebrained kid. Even Pa hardly paid any attention to what he said. Big Stan had practically threatened him to keep his mouth shut. But he was thinking, if he could lure Sammy into some act that would betray his real character—? Jeff thought of Ben Thurston and that beating. He wondered if one of those masked men had maybe had blond curly hair?

It was a painful prospect, to offer himself as a target

for a roughing-up, but Jeff reassured himself that he'd have to plan it some foolproof way, so that witnesses would rush in before he could get hurt. And it bolstered his nerve considerably to reflect that if he did manage to bring it off, it would certainly make him—well, maybe not a hero, but at least the object of some respect, even from Ben Thurston. They could hardly call him "dummy" after he'd showed up a Company spy!

"Well, well, well." Sammy slapped an arm across Jeff's shoulders with all the gentle affection of a grizzly cuffing its young. "Another day, another dollar, eh? First hundred years is the hardest, eh? How's tricks, Jeffie-boy?"

It was so different from his growlish tone the night before that Jeff stiffened with instant mistrust.

"I'm doing O.K.," he answered roughly. "How goes it with you, Sammy?"

"Fine. Great. But then I got a pretty good job—got no boss like Big Stan lookin' down my neck. Even the pit boss don't bother me."

"Big Stan's all right," Jeff said tensely, feeling the full burden of that powerful arm across his back and trying not to scringe under it.

"Sounded to me like he was givin' you a hard time back there in the washhouse," Sammy went on, friendly as all get-out. "He's got no right to pick on you after the whistle blows. Any time you want him took down a peg, just let me know, Jeffie-boy."

"Jeffie-boy" gritted his teeth. "Why should you do that for me, Sammy?" he inquired innocently.

60

"Well, because. I mean we gotta stick together, what with me sparkin' your sis and all. Now you just tell me what that was all about in the showers just now, and I'll see those guys don't bully you no more. Seemed to me they were tryin' to make out like you're too young to know what's going on, eh?"

"Who cares?" Jeff tried to shrug, but couldn't, with two tons bearing down on his shoulders.

"And you was tellin' 'em quite proper that you know a-plenty about what goes on. Of course, you ain't tellin' them nothin', because you don't owe them a thing, right? What they ever done for you, right? A boy with a sis as smart as you got, he's got to be pretty smart too, the way I figure."

Jeff's heart was pumping fear into his throat, but he managed to say, offhand, "Well, I keep my eyes open."

"Sure you do! And you keep your mouth shut—I heard you say so up there in the washhouse. Good boy. You'll get ahead, just like me. I'm gonna get ahead—ain't nobody gonna stop me. And if, like it looks, you and me are all in the same family someday, I'm gonna see to it that you do all right, too. I can give you some tips, you can give me some, maybe. . . ."

It began to get across to Jeff what Sammy was trying to suggest. And as it dawned—that Sammy was actually trying to interest him in turning spy himself—Jeff got so mad he got careless.

"There's some ways of getting ahead that I wouldn't tie up to with forty feet of line," he said bluntly.

The amount of silence that came from Sammy in

the wake of that remark started the boy to trembling inside again. He was botching this, just as he'd done in the showers. He needed more time, to plan a cool, smooth approach. They had reached the Row now, were right in front of McNish's store.

"Well, so long," he said purposefully, "I've got to go in here and buy some—some carbide for Pa."

"I need a few things, myself," said Yates, with equal firmness. And together they went up the steps, though Sammy did let go the steely grip on the boy's shoulder.

Jeff noticed uncomfortably that his companion didn't seem about to buy anything. While they waited for McNish to weigh out a pound of carbide, the big blond man reached into the open drum and picked up a few grains of the stuff. In his calloused palm, it lay like small gray gravel.

"You'll be buyin' this for yourself one of these days," he remarked, with mock regret. "I'll bet you'll buy a thousand pounds in all them years you'll be diggin' coal."

That was probably true enough. Every miner had his own supply of the near-magic material, for it was that which gave them the only light they had down in the dark reaches of the mine. Just this and water, a drop at a time dripping from the top half of the container onto the carbide in the bottom half—this ingenious device made up each miner's headlamp. The water, working on the carbide, formed a gas which could be lit, and that tiny fierce blue flame burning in the center of its reflector was all that stood between a miner and the absolute blackness under the earth—sometimes the only "sun" a man had for weeks on end.

Jeff drew a long breath. "Yep," he said, "I reckon I'll be needing it, all right."

"Unless, like I said, a feller gets ahead, figures it smart. You don't really have to grub in a hole all your life, I always say." Sammy lowered his voice. "Me, I aim to get out, get me a job up-top, live in a good-looking house. That's why I got to have me a good-looking gal —" He dug an elbow into Jeff's ribs hard enough to bust one.

McNish came back with the sack of carbide. A scrawny, oldish man with thin red hair, he handed the purchase to Jeff and marked it down in his cramped little writing in the ledger beside the cash register.

"Pretty tough," murmured Sammy as they moved away, "always got them figures addin' up against your name. You stay down in the shaft, though, and you ain't never gonna get even on McNish's black book, that's sure."

Jeff dawdled along the counters of clothing, heavy overalls, Levis, the clumsy shoes and thick gloves. He was wishing Sammy would go home, but the big man stuck like a mustard plaster.

"Gets awful cold down below, come winter," he was going on solemnly. "Them clothes weigh a man down somethin' turrible. You ever been down the slope, Jeff-boy?"

"No." Jeff had hinted and even nagged at his father for a chance to go below, just to see what it was like down there, but he'd been turned down flat every time.

"Listen." Sammy backed him up between the rows of stovepipe and bolts of dress goods. Jeff was beginning to squirm—miners were drifting into the store and he didn't want to be seen with Sammy. "Listen, boy, I'd like to do you a favor. And maybe you'll do one for me some time—put in a good word with your sis, you know, tell her I'm on your side, eh? Maybe you and me could help each other a lot. What's wrong with that?"

"I don't want any favors, Sammy," Jeff protested.

"Oh, I didn't mean any real big thing. I just thought —well, you owe it to yourself to see what it's like down below. After all, you're gonna spend a long time down there. And I'm gonna see if I can fix it so's you can come down, maybe help me out one of these days. How'd that be? Not so bad, eh—get off the picking table awhile, mess around with the horses instead? It'll give you an idea, a real idea, how it's gonna be down there, all them years ahead of you. And then maybe we can have a little talk, eh?"

Jeff still didn't like the undertone of conspiracy, but he thought he'd better play along, at least for right now. And he really didn't have to pretend much as he said, "Well, that would be interesting, all right. I wouldn't mind that at all."

"That's-a-boy!" Sammy grinned. "You'n me, we'll make out good yet!"

7

When Jeff looked up from the picking table next morning and saw Sammy Yates talking to Big Stan, he ducked his head and concentrated hard on his work. Much as it was a pleasant thought, to be rescued from the tipple for a while, he certainly wasn't ready yet for that "little talk" with Sammy.

He had gone to bed the night before determined to plot a good course of action, but he'd fallen asleep before he even knew it was happening. Now, when the hand tapped his shoulder, he groaned inwardly and wished he had kept awake, tired or not. Big Stan didn't look much pleased as he beckoned Jeff on out into the sunlight where Sammy stood waiting.

"Yeah, there's my boy." Yates nodded. "I tell you, I've seen him work around the livery stable—he's got a good hand with horses."

That was somewhat of an exaggeration, but Jeff really had hung around the stable quite a bit in those golden days before he had to go to work.

"Now, listen," Big Stan was instructing him, loud and slow. "Sammy here, he got his foot stepped on by a horse, so he needs some help over the noon hour. You do what-all he says, and you can get your lunch when you come back up. And make sure *you* don't get your foot mashed, understand?"

"Yes, sir." Jeff nodded unhappily. As he went along with Sammy, who made a big show of limping, the blond man gave him a knowing wink.

A string of empty coal cars stood on a switch near the mine entrance, waiting to be taken down; the two of them climbed into one. As they settled down, Sammy grinned openly.

"That wasn't hard a-tall," he said. "You just gotta know how to go about these things. Oh, I could show you a-plenty."

Jeff squirmed for a more comfortable seat on the bare bottom of the car. "I hope Pa doesn't catch me down there. He's against kids—younger fellows, I mean—going below."

"Well, now, maybe your pa don't have nothin' to say about this," Sammy told him loftily. "How'd you like to be set up so's you wouldn't never have to take orders from your old man again?"

It was an interesting speculation, but for some reason it didn't fill Jeff with as much pleasure as he would have thought.

"Just one little item we got to get straight, though. Right now." Sammy spoke with sudden purpose. "Just so's we know where we both stand, you tell me: Where was you night before last, and what-all did you see—if you seen anything?"

The question was put so abruptly it caught Jeff unaware. He felt himself flush with guilty understanding—felt that the answer must be written all over his face for the probing eyes to read. Sammy had yellowish eyes—something like those of a lynx cat. Swiftly it was borne in on Jeff that Sammy was already fairly sure of the truth; he decided to bluff it through, try a counterattack of his own.

"Night before last?" he repeated. "Oh, I reckon I must have seen a lot of things. Wasn't that the night I ran into you, out on the bench?"

"Why, so it was! I thought maybe you'd forgot that. Big question is, who—what else—did you maybe see?"

Jeff hesitated, trying to think of a good answer.

Sammy grinned hopefully. "I think maybe you *did* forget, by jing! They say it's a dummy that forgets, but I say it takes brains, real brains, to forget the right things. Eh? How about that, Jeff-boy?"

Jeff felt a twinge of excitement—the zest of combat. As carefully as if he were taking aim at somebody else's taw, he said, "I don't know. . . . Ben Thurston says it takes more brains to ask questions."

67

"So I've heard." Sammy nodded gravely. "I heard, too, that he got beat somethin' turrible on account of all them questions. Gettin' whipped with a length of chain must hurt fierce."

Jeff swallowed dryly. He was almost sure that Thurston hadn't mentioned the nature of his treatment to anybody else in Bearcat. Nobody but Jeff seemed to know any details of it at all—if they had, they'd all have been hashing it over. And he himself certainly hadn't told anyone. So if Sammy knew about the chain—?

Those tawny eyes were digging into him. It was almost as if Sammy realized he'd made a slip. Jeff was trembling inside, but then this was what he had planned to do—to lay himself out as bait in his own trap. Now, all he had to do was figure a way to get Sammy to jump him just at the right time, with miners on the scene to step in before Jeff could take much damage— That was going to take a little planning, and, until he had it worked out, he was thinking he'd better stick close to home of nights.

As the two sat measuring each other warily, the switchman came over to their string of empties, glanced at his two passengers, and coupled the big cable onto the end car. Releasing the brake, he gave the signal to the man up in the powerhouse, which was on slightly raised ground above the entrance of the mine. Jeff saw the operator up there throw a lever, and the cable began to haul the train slowly up off the siding and onto the main track. Through the window of the powerhouse, he could see the windlass turning, winding the cable up

68

onto a giant spool, as they were drawn up, backward, until the whole string of cars was clear of the siding and Jeff was looking down a long incline into the black mouth of the mine.

"Keep your head low, boy," called the switchman, and gave the "down" signal.

It was as if the cable had snapped. The cars seemed to roll free-wheel toward the square of darkness—they plunged into it, still picking up speed, rattling, bucketing along, tearing down the steep, pitch-dark slope faster and faster, with the jagged roof of the tunnel so close overhead that Jeff could feel the rush of it just inches away. He crouched on the floor of the car, motionless —he'd heard of men who had got careless and had their heads literally torn off in that slashing descent. But nothing he'd ever been told could have described the awful sense of plunging out of control into a bottomless pit.

Coal smell deepened as they went down, and a dank chill cut through his shirt. Jeff's ears felt as if they'd been plugged with cotton. And then, some thousands of feet in the ground, something began to check their wild pace—the cable grabbed and slowed them, little by little, until they rolled out smoothly onto the broad floor of a big rocky cavern, flickeringly lighted with kerosene lamps.

"Are we at the bottom?" asked Jeff weakly.

Sammy snickered. "Just the first level, Jeffie-boy. What's the matter, leave your stomick up-top?" He flipped a breezy salute to the switchman and swung

down out of the car. Jeff noticed that he'd forgotten to
limp.

"Come on over, take a look at my layout," he said,
heading toward a row of stalls built along one of the
hewn rock walls of the big underground room.

Jeff, trailing him, glanced back to see the switchman
reach up, jerk twice on a cord strung overhead along
the track. Up and down the slope, little bells ding-
dinged, and the string of empties slid forward again,
over the brink of the slope to drop away into the deeper
regions of the mine.

His father, he knew, was clear down on the third
level. He wondered who was working this one. The
sidings that crisscrossed the floor were empty of cars,
and so were the tracks leading off toward the dark
openings around the edges—the mouths of the entries.
The tunnels seemed unearthly quiet. Jeff's own steps
sounded loud against the low ceiling of rock, as he
followed Sammy over to the stalls.

There were only two horses tethered there, ponderous heavy beasts that stood hipshot and stared straight
ahead at nothing, as if reconciled to their gloomy surroundings. Even though Jeff knew they were used in
shifts and walked up the slope after a month below, to
roam the pasture for a full week of rest, he still felt
sorry for the passive animals. He tried to imagine what
they must feel, shut in down here day and night, made
to haul the heavy, loaded cars out of the entries to the
main track, hour after hour.

Again he glanced around at the silent passageways leading off into darkness. "Where are the rest of the horses?" he asked, his voice sounding hollow in the vault of the room.

"Oh, they're all below, on second and third levels," Sammy told him. "This level's mined out. There ain't no men workin' here no more."

That gave Jeff a skipped heartbeat. He hadn't reckoned on being alone with Sammy—not yet! Keeping well out of the burly man's reach, he glanced around, beginning at once to plan a way of escape in case Sammy should start something. Best chance was to run down the slope to the next level, probably, if he didn't meet a string of coal cars coming up.

But the stable boss was paying hardly any attention to him. Over by the big bin of oats, he was measuring out grain into a row of nosebags, talking along.

"So—you and me got to carry the grub down to our long-tailed cousins, and while I'm doing this, you could go in the tack room yonder and find my leather punch —it's hangin' on the wall—and pick out some scraps of good thick mendin' leather. They tell me there's a piece of harness broke, down on third level."

Jeff was glad enough to be put to work at something removed from Sammy's vicinity. He went into the wooden shed built against the far wall. The odor of sweat-soaked leather was strong enough to drown out some of the coal smell, and Jeff even welcomed it. He took his time grubbing through piles of broken harness to find several loose ends of straps, finally located the leather punch. When he went back out, Sammy was just finishing with the grain.

"Now take a couple of these and give 'em to those poor old nags over there—they're too lame to work." He jerked a thumb at the stalls, then stopped abruptly and cussed. "Doggone it! She's done it again!"

Jeff saw that there was only one horse there now. In the other stall hung a piece of frayed rope.

"That ornery, wall-eyed mare, she saws around so much, she works through every halter I put on her," Sammy grumbled. "Now I got to go hunt her before we can leave for downstairs. Can't let her just wander around the entries, she'd be knockin' down timber." He picked up one of the many lighted lanterns that hung from hooks around the walls. "You may as well help," he added over his shoulder. "Take a light and look down Number One entry—that one there. I'll take Number Two." He was already heading down one of the gloomy tunnels.

Jeff helped himself to a lamp and approached Number One entry with a certain reluctance. Its foul-smelling depths stretched away like the maw of a worm, crooking out of sight ahead, swallowing the yellow light of the lantern as he advanced along it cautiously.

It was an old entry, probably the oldest in the mine. The tracks had even been taken up from it. In places the tunnel had been cut through loose rock, which was held back by a crude framework of timbers through which water dripped. The rough-hewn logs that formed the ceiling were held in place by uprights that had been wedged in tight on either end, but where the wood had begun to rot they didn't look too tight any more, and the whole top roofing of the entry was swaybacked under the weight of tons of rock. One small kick from a horse really could knock out a post and bring the whole works down.

Jeff eyed the rickety structure anxiously as he proceeded, around one twist in the tunnel after another—for an entry must follow the vein of coal, no matter what direction it takes.

And then abruptly he stopped still. He'd just passed a pool where the stinking stagnant water had collected, and it occurred to him to wonder why a horse would want to go down a foul, close corridor like this. Piling on top of that came another question—how could anything that big sneak out of a stall and wander away without Sammy hearing it or noticing?

Standing still, hardly breathing, Jeff listened—for what, he wasn't sure. Something too small to be heard. Out of the corner of his eye, he caught the slightest movement in the shadows along the ground, almost like a snake. Holding the light down, he saw what it was— a rope, an old dirty hemp rope that strung along the floor of the tunnel as far back and ahead as he could make out. Even as he watched, it moved again, tightened as if someone had picked it up and was pulling. . . .

Jeff didn't wait to see what it was attached to. He turned and ran. Back along the entry he flung himself pell-mell, caroming off the walls as he rounded corners, the lantern swinging crazily. Behind him, he heard a terrible sound—the crack of wood giving way, followed by the deafening roar of a cave-in. It spread, racing after him as one patch of collapsing timber carried the next down with it. A choking cloud of dust caught up with him—the creak and stress was all around now, over his head. He heard a new splintering of rotten wood, and as he plunged on rocks began to fall in front of him. Then—the whole mountain seemed to come down in a crash of darkness.

8

*I*t took Jeff a few seconds to realize that he was still conscious. The wind had been knocked out of him so hard he thought he was going to die of suffocation. When he did manage to get his lungs working, he could take only the least shallow breath. The weight of rock on him held him motionless, spread-eagled face down—he couldn't even move his hands. As his mind cleared, he realized that a big timber had wedged just over his head—he could feel the edge of it, but not the weight. And it was this that had kept the rock from piling in around his face, saving a little pocket of air. But it wasn't much—probably not enough to last until somebody dug him out. *If* they dug him out.

The glassy-clear logic of his reasoning surprised him. Gripped in deathly fear, Jeff found he could still think with gruesome accuracy. He almost wished he had been knocked out—he didn't really want to know what it would be like when there wasn't any more air to breathe.

And nobody even knew he was under here except Sammy. Figured wrong again . . . thought Sammy could be fooled around with, tricked . . . Thurston would laugh . . . *you're an amateur* . . . except that Jeff knew he wouldn't laugh, not over a thing like this. And Pa? How would he ever know . . . ? Except that somehow, an accident . . .

Jeff tried not to breathe so fast. It was making his ears ring. Or was it true—did he really hear, far away, a little rapid ding-ding-ding-ding-ding, as if somebody were yanking fast on the railroad signal rope? And then —no doubt about it—he felt, through the rock floor, the pound of footsteps running.

Voices came through to him, so the rock slide must have halted shortly after it took him down. That meant there was a chance— Jeff tried again to wriggle a little but only felt more sickeningly the terrible pressure piled on top of him.

"I tell you, just as it came down I heard a yell," said somebody.

Jeff hadn't realized that he'd cried out.

"I didn't hear nothin'." That was Sammy.

"Look. What's under that timber? Looks like a busted lantern."

"Say, you're right. It sure does." Sammy sounded

76

innocent as sweet violets.

With a surge of desperation, Jeff tried to call out—only drew in a mouthful of rock dust. Choking, he felt a burst of terror. The miners used to talk of it: *If you get caught under rock, don't lose your head and try to holler. Lie still and pray.* Jeff made himself quiet down inside; carefully he spit out the grit and in a few seconds he could breathe a little again.

They were still talking. Somebody else had come up now—Jeff thought it must be the switchman.

"Where's that kid, the picker you brought down here?"

"By George, I ain't seen him!" Sammy sounded shocked. "You reckon that little varmint strayed off down that entry? He was dyin' to go explorin', but I told him, you stick right here and do like you're told. . . ."

"Don't stand there blabberin'. Dig!"

And Jeff heard the welcome sound of rocks being tossed aside. More men were coming now; the tunnel was full of their voices.

"I sure hope he ain't deep back in there," Sammy was saying. "I bet that fall goes clear back to the weak spot. Remember that bad place where they had to shore up the roof with a center-post?"

Jeff thought, oh yes. That post was probably what you jerked out, good old Sammy-boy, just about the time you figured I'd be under the weak spot. And if he'd really been caught back there, Jeff knew his bones would lie unfound for the next million years.

"Of course, if you do find him, poor dern little idiot'll

be dead," Sammy told them helpfully.

But nobody stopped digging. If anything, it sounded as though they were going at it harder. And a minute later, the weight on Jeff's arms began to lighten.

"That's his shirt! It's him!"

They dug frantically now; the loose dirt was scraped away from around his head, and Jeff saw light. The most blindingly beautiful thing he'd ever laid eyes on, that yellow flutter. He blinked, and through the men went a gasp of relief.

"The kid's alive!"

"Good boy! Didn't panic. Lie still, sonny—"

"We'll have you out of there quick."

"Be careful, he may be hurt bad."

That hadn't occurred to Jeff. He'd felt numb ever since the rock hit. Now a whole new fear swam over him.

"Look. Them timbers are wedged against the wall like jackstraws. Must have held the worst of the big rock off him."

"Don't disturb them beams. See if you can't snake him out."

Little by little, Jeff felt himself dragged free, though the press of the cave-in tore the overalls almost off him and scraped a good deal of skin.

"That was a close one," somebody said shakily.

"Better not turn him over till Doc gets here."

"Jeff!" It was his father, kneeling at his side. In the lantern light, the lean irregular face was haunted with shadows. "How bad you hurt, son?"

It had been a long time since Pa had called him that.

"You mean he's really alive?" Sammy was demanding. Jeff thought he sounded scared now. "Well—that's —that's good. I mean, I told him and told him not to go near them entries!"

Still lying face down, Jeff was finding it almost as hard to breathe as before, but he managed to rally enough strength to say, "Pa." It came out a whisper; he couldn't seem to make it any louder.

Harry Danver put his ear down close.

Quickly Jeff gasped, "Sammy did it on purpose . . . sent me in there. . . ." And that was all he could manage.

"What did he say?"

Danver straightened up. In a dead-pan voice, he said, "Boy wants some water. Sammy, where do you keep that drinking water for the hosses?"

"I'll get some." Yates went off in a hurry.

Pa drew down close again, and the men, sensing something, grew still.

"Now tell, if you can. Why did he send you?"

With an effort, Jeff whispered. "On account . . . I found out he's . . . Regan's spy."

"How do you know?" his father urged softly.

"Saw him . . . at Regan's house." With one last bit of strength, Jeff added, "Is the rope . . . still there?"

"What rope?"

"Rope he pulled down the rock with."

Danver looked up and spoke to the men in a low voice; Jeff heard him repeat it all, word for word. "Looks like we caught ourselves a spy," he finished. "Now if we can find that rope—"

Several of them went off to the edge of the rubble. "No rope here now."

"Sammy wouldn't have left it. He'd have pulled it out or cut it off."

"It's under a million tons of rock now—we'll never prove a thing on him."

"I don't care!" With sudden suppressed fury, Danver spoke out. "If that's the way Regan wants to play, I reckon we can play rough, too!"

And somebody else started, "Let's get that stool pigeon...!"

"Ssssh!" Another hushed him. "Here comes Zack."

Zack was the pit boss. "What the sam-hill's going on?" he demanded. "Why should Yates bring a kid down here? Where is Sammy, anyhow?"

"Looks like he made hisself scarce," commented one of the miners dryly. "He's not out at the stable."

What didn't make sense to Zack was adding up bigger every minute to the men. Jeff could feel it building.

"Did the boy say anything—?" the pit boss began, but before he could press that question, there was a rattle of cars out on the track as a train of empties came down, and a minute later the doctor pushed through the crowd.

"Looks like the whole blasted town has got itself packed into this tunnel," he snapped irritably. "Stand back!"

Bending over Jeff, he held one of the lanterns to shine in the boy's eyes. "Move your right hand . . . your left. . . . That's it. Now try to move your feet. Good." He ran his fingers lightly over Jeff's body.

80

"Back's not broken. Looks like he got off with only a couple of ribs cracked, dislocated collarbone. That's all, near as I can tell, but we'll have to get him up-top before I can do any more. Bring those blankets, somebody—"

As several of the men helped roll Jeff onto an improvised stretcher, Zack started off.

"I've got to make a report on this. The rest of you get back to work." And then he stopped, for a strange thing was happening.

Lying on his back now, Jeff could see it—almost like a current of determination, eddying through the crowd of men. They stood dogged and unmoving, in spite of Zack's orders.

The pit boss looked around at them uneasily. "What's ailing the lot of you?"

Harry Danver spoke up hoarsely. "Nothing's the matter, Zack. Just a hurt kid. Just one more accident, like happens all the time. It could've been any of us, only it wasn't—it was a boy that ain't turned man yet. And it happened under orders."

"Well now, who said—did he say he was ordered? Well, I'll have to ask Sammy a few questions, but—" Zack's voice petered out on him. "Anyhow, we got him out, that's the main thing," he added heartily.

"*We* got him out," said one of the miners quietly, "and me, I'm gonna go along and just see that he gets home O.K."

"Me, too," chimed in another.

And as Danver and the doctor carried Jeff out to the

81

tracks, the men grouped in solidly around them.

"It don't take the whole blamed shift to carry the boy home!" Zack spoke sharply, but he stood aside and didn't get in their path. "This is crazy! You can't just walk off your jobs!"

Without a word, the men climbed into the string of empty coal cars, crowding together, watchful and silent. The switchman reached for the signal rope, pulled it three times—all along the length the bells jangled. Slowly the train moved up into the darkness of the slope.

Zack followed a few steps, helplessly. "You want me to tell Regan you all just—left?" he shouted.

From the cars, someone called back, "Tell Regan if he wants trouble, we'll give it to him."

Jeff looked up at the men crouched around him in the car. They were all familiar faces, but somehow different, too. Maybe it was the downward shed of light from each miner's lamp that wrote the contours of their features in such hard lines. They looked as grim and set as if they'd been hacked out of the mountain itself. His father's jaw was squared off hard as a block of building stone.

Once Pa glanced down at him curiously. "You done all right in this," he said, almost with pride.

And Jeff could even enjoy the ache of his bruised body. The whole shift, going up-top to see him home, walking off work—if it wasn't exactly as he'd planned it . . . still, being a hero was not half bad.

82

Part II
The Fire

9

*U*nder a mild afternoon sun, the Row looked almost peaceful. Women meandered along the street—it was a little muddy from last night's thunder-shower; they stepped carefully but went right on with their gossip. As usual, a line of loafers sat on the hitch-rack in front of the stable, old codgers who couldn't work any more. A few newcomers strolled the town—quite a few. But in summer there were bound to be drifters. That was nothing to get disturbed about, not really.

Behind the tipple, smoke rose from the slag dump and curled in the lazy air. Sometimes a stir of wind would send a faint thread of it down toward the Row

—a nose-wrinkling stench of coal fumes. For the dump always smoldered, down underneath. And on quiet days like this, the gases would collect until a fan of wind came along to make them flare, sometimes sending a rush of blue flame sweeping over the whole dump.

The mine itself stood idle. There had been no work all week. This was common enough in summertime; nobody would have questioned a layoff if it hadn't been that particular week, after the shift had walked out. And yet nobody had been fired. Everything was quiet in Bearcat. So it was hard to put a finger on the strange underlying tension—a wariness that was tightening around the town like a noose.

"I don't like it," said the Deacon plaintively. "Suspicion, fear, hatred—neighbor against neighbor—it's sinful, my friends. These passions should never be loosed abroad." Solemnly he looked around at his small audience, grouped in the Danvers' front room.

Ma stood in the kitchen doorway, kneading the skirt of her apron nervously. It wasn't often she had a caller as important as the Deacon. Becky, perched on a straight chair near the bedroom door, shucked the baby up and down gently on her lap to keep it quiet. Over on the sofa sat Pa, just as he'd sat most of this week, hunched forward over his knees, silent and figuring. And on a cot set up beside the front window lay the object of the Deacon's unexpected visit.

Propped against the pillows, Jeff fidgeted. He felt as if big things were about to happen, and here he was, pinned down to a bed, too remote to be part of them. Right now he sensed an uneasiness gathering around that last remark of the Deacon's which still hung ominously in the air. Passions abroad. It had been this way all week —every word that anybody said seemed to cloak a powerful meaning.

Danver was prickled, too. "What you getting at, Deacon? We haven't turned neighbor agin neighbor."

"Brother, I was thinking of this poor rogue, Yates, whose negligence caused this lamentable accident. I understand he has fled from town."

Pa nodded. "I reckon he flew the coop, all right. Leastways nobody's seen him. And begging your pardon, Deacon, it wasn't carelessness. It was cold-blooded murdering he had on his mind, and if that works up a soreness in me, I reckon I can't help it."

"And yet a week ago, he was your neighbor." The Deacon shook his head sadly. "No matter how guilty Yates may be, friends, your suspicion hurts you and everybody else. The whole town will wonder—*who may be next?* Oh, good people, this is an unhappy way to live. We must put ill will from us . . ."

"Well, how?" Ma blurted out. "When folks get to spyin' and deceivin', how can you help but keep a watch out, Deacon? What else is to do?"

"Patience, dear sister. We could all learn a lesson from this poor simple-minded child." The Deacon laid one of his pink, clean hands on Jeff's knee. "It's outright gladdening to see how meekly he bears his afflic-

87

tions." There was nothing but kindliness in that chubby face with its beautiful dark eyes, and yet the words fretted Jeff like sandpaper.

It had not been so consarned simple-minded to handle Sammy as skillfully as he'd done—except for that one slight mistake of going down the entry. All this week Jeff had been enjoying a certain increase in everybody's respect, especially his father's. Pa spoke quietly to him these days and kept watching him in that guarded way, as if the boy, too, were part of something he was trying to solve.

The rest of the miners had made a real fuss over the invalid all week, but Jeff was forced to admit that it wasn't so much a personal thing with them. It was just that they were all concentrating their own resentments into one big anger centered around him. It was as if they needed a rallying point. Ever since the day they had stood together to walk out, they had been almost afraid of their own decision. And the longer the layoff lasted, the deeper the fear was driven. So they came to recharge their spirits by the sight of Jeff all taped and bandaged. And if they didn't exactly set him up as the brightest kid in town, at least it had been a whole week since anybody had called him "dummy." Now, to have the Deacon revert to it was disheartening.

"I don't feel very afflicted," he protested irritably.

"Deacon just said you was bein' good and meek," Ma admonished, "so, be."

All at once, Pa took issue. "I don't know about that." He clapped his hands on his knees and sat up straight.

"I ain't so sure it's fitting to sit patient when somebody's tried to kill a man—not even a man, just a kid. I been thinking about it."

"I know, Brother Danver, I can see hatred growing on you like moss." The Deacon spoke kindly but his face was stern. "If it's true that there was evil intent in poor Yates, he'll pay the penalty when he stands up on Judgment Day for the great reckoning. But I say you're making it hard on yourself to carry the kernel of bitterness in your soul. Next thing, you'll start thinking: Who else is a traitor? You'll start to suspect this man and that, you'll say: There had to be more than one spy—"

"You are sure right," Danver admitted doggedly. "I know plumb well there's got to be others. Question is, how to find them out."

"And when an ordinary mortal man tries to take over the work of heavenly judgment, innocent people can get hurt," the Deacon warned. "Then all men are at the mercy of any spiteful person who may spread lies, any child who claims to have seen something. . . ."

"You trying to say Jeff didn't see Sammy Yates coming out of Pete Regan's house?" Pa eyed the Deacon straight, as if he were just any man.

"No, no." The Deacon smiled tolerantly. "I'm only saying that another boy could have fabricated the whole scene, or enlarged it. He could have imagined, for instance, that he saw two or three men in Mr. Regan's house."

"Well, I did," Jeff admitted. "I saw two."

The Deacon looked pained, as if everything was turning out just as he feared.

Danver stared blankly. "Why in tarnation didn't you say so before?"

"I couldn't make out who the other one was, but there were two."

"I didn't think that Sammy could've rigged that accident without being told how," Pa mused. "He's not smart enough. I'd say there's somebody with sharp brains at the bottom of this."

"Tut, sir, you indict every intelligent man in town," the Deacon said, shocked. With a sigh he stood up to go. "Just such an unfortunate train of thought may have led to the misfortunes of our schoolmaster, who, I hear, was recently manhandled by persons unknown. Terrible business—if the man is as blameless as he pretends. Oh, judge not, good friends. Counsel your neighbors to peace. Remember that violence only creates answering violence, and then innocents may be hurt." He laid a hand on Jeff's head lightly. "Good afternoon, friends. When you feel the need of help, I beg of you, call on me."

After he had gone, Pa sat rubbing a hand over the gray stubble on his jaw.

Ma sighed. "I declare, it makes sense, about how anybody can put out a mean word and suspicion a person's name—"

"Well, think about it good," Pa told her, "and you and the other females keep a closer mouth when you're in McNish's."

That sent her off to the kitchen with a swish of skirts.

Becky got up, too, but Pa said, "Wait a minute."

She stood, dutiful and quiet. It wasn't the first time he had turned to her for help. Becky could always put a different slant on a question.

Ponderously, Danver said, "I'm thought-out. I hear things and I don't lay hold of 'em. Becky, what was the Deacon getting at about the teacher? Thurston's on our side, ain't he?"

"I don't know Ben Thurston," Becky said slowly, "but he's only been in town since last fall and he's an Easterner, likely never set foot in a mine in his life. Why should he be on our side?"

"Well, everybody knows he's been getting under Regan's skin, else why did Pete send men to rough him up?"

"Nobody knows who sent them." She shook her head. "Besides, if Mr. Regan doesn't like him, why doesn't he just fire him?"

Pa looked at her, puzzled. "You know, I been wondering that myself. You don't reckon it could've been the teacher that Jeff saw—?"

Jeff was smarting under a disappointment of his own. All this week, the teacher hadn't even come to pay his respects. Now, daring to break in on his father's conversation, he said, "Becky, why did you tell me once to stay clear of Mr. Thurston?"

She looked at them shyly, as if reluctant to put her notion into words. "It's just—like the Deacon says—

trouble gets more trouble. And when I look at Ben Thurston, I feel it hanging over him like fox fire."

Jeff thought, dryly, that he couldn't see anything hanging over Thurston as the schoolmaster walked up the Row that next morning. From his post at the front window, the boy had a good view of the street; the air was almighty clear, too, what with the mine laid off and no smoke pouring from the boilerhouse. So it would have been a good time to catch this flicker of danger that Becky had spoken of. And yet Jeff saw only a tall young man swinging along at that easy stride of his. He was bareheaded, his straight brown hair coming a little loose in the light breeze. The lean face was wearing its usual look—pleasant, but straight-lipped and watchful. One of the things that made some folks uneasy about Thurston was that he smiled so seldom.

As the teacher turned in at their gate and came purposefully to the house, Jeff tightened up for a battle —some sort of battle. Maybe it was this that Becky had meant, this challenge that Thurston always seemed ready to throw down.

There was no one around but Jeff just then; Ma and the twins were at the store, Pa had gone off around the Row to talk to his cronies, and Becky was tending the baby in the back of the house somewhere. So when Thurston knocked, Jeff could only call out to him.

"Come in—the door's unlatched."

A little diffidently, the schoolmaster accepted the invitation and stepped inside; he hesitated, to survey the boy on the cot. Finally, coming over to Jeff's side, he said, with evident concern, "Do you really feel well enough to see me?"

"Everybody else in town has been over here," Jeff informed him.

"I know that. But it's harder to talk to a sworn enemy." And all at once, Thurston cracked off one of those rare smiles that was nearly as straight across as if it had been passed between two boys the same age. Sitting down at Jeff's side, he took a book from under his arm and tossed it onto the bed.

"For your convalescence," he explained. "Written by your namesake a hundred years ago. You really ought to read it, if you can."

Stung by the implication, Jeff picked it up. *The Collected Letters of Thomas Jefferson.* A fine dull schoolish thing to lend him. Probably ask for a book report on it. . . . And then, as he glanced inside the cover, he was brought up short. Under the teacher's own name, written there long ago, he saw something penned in newer ink:

For Jeff—
  "Time now begins to be precious to you." Good luck, and good use of it.
                                    Ben

"That quotation, incidentally, is from the book itself," Thurston added. "Written by a great man to a young student."

"You're giving me—?" Jeff broke off unhappily. Books cost money! There had never been one in the Danvers' house, except spellers and primers and that sort of drivel. To have the teacher give him a thing of value made Jeff uncomfortable.

"I don't believe in lending," Thurston told him. "Besides, it may be years before you feel up to reading it. I hope you do, someday—there's a deal of common sense all through the letters and if anybody ever needed that, you do. From what I hear, you almost tom-fooled yourself out of existence this time."

Jeff stared at him, speechless with indignation.

"Well, didn't you? Let me review the facts as I've been told them," Thurston offered. "Set me right if I'm wrong. You chanced on a meeting which you should have known was as explosive as black powder. Instead of speaking up to your father and keeping quiet in front of the conspirator, you apparently did just the opposite, making sure that he knew you had discovered his double-dealing game. Then you allowed this dangerous person to lure you into a deserted spot, even cooperated with him to put yourself in a position so that he could pull the mine down around you—"

"I didn't!" yelled Jeff furiously. "I got out of there! I guessed what he was up to and I thought fast, and I kept my head when I was under a couple of tons of rock! I'd just like to see—some other people—get buried by a cave-in!"

Thurston nodded matter-of-factly. "You mean me.

94

Well, I agree that it would not be easy to keep from reacting wildly under those conditions. Much easier—and more healthy—to avoid being trapped in such a situation."

"You didn't avoid getting beat up!"

"Score one for you. But you must admit I had less choice in the matter. Or wasn't it true that you went along amicably with Sammy Yates?"

Jeff didn't know or care about amick-whatever-it-was. He was so rigid with outrage that his broken ribs were beginning to ache.

"Why did you come here? To make me feel worse?" he yelled.

"Yes, why did you come, Mr. Thurston?" Becky stood in the doorway, straight as a young aspen. Jeff had never seen her so angry. It made her prettier than usual, the color in her cheeks and the blaze of her crystal-gray eyes.

Ben Thurston got slowly to his feet and stood speechless for a minute. Then, without taking his eyes off her, he spoke to Jeff.

"Will you do me the kindness to introduce me to your sister?"

"I'm Becky Danver," she said, walking forward to stand beside the cot, as if to protect the boy. "Why should he do you a kindness, Mr. Thurston? What have you done for him?"

"Not enough," replied the teacher readily. "Which answers your question as to why I came here today."

95

"You came to badger a poor injured child."

"And to let him badger me, of course," added Thurston. "That's part of the ground rules, since he's out of school now, isn't it, Jeff?"

This seemed to disconcert Becky. Or maybe it was the easy way he answered her, all the while studying her with open pleasure.

"That's no fair exchange," she retorted, flushing. "He's just a boy and not—" She checked herself quickly, but Jeff knew what she'd been about to say.

So did Thurston. "There seems to be some talk that Jeff's not very bright. He was just now telling me the opposite. In fact, he was shouting at me that he was a pretty smart fellow, smarter than I am. If you hadn't intervened, Miss Becky, he might even have convinced me, who knows?" There was a quirk of humor at the corners of his straight-set mouth.

"Oh, for shame!" Becky reproached him sharply. "To make sport of the boy! Don't you see how it can hurt?"

Thurston shoved his hands in his pockets and paced across to stare out the window a minute. When he turned and came back, there was no more amusement in his eyes. He seemed tired as he looked down at Jeff.

For no apparent reason, he asked, "Did it hurt when the doctor set that collarbone, Jeff?" Then he glanced up at Becky. "Would it have been kinder to let the boy go on suffering a dislocation?"

Puzzled, Jeff glanced up at his sister, who stood there as wide-eyed as if she'd been pricked by a pin. Then

96

the stiffness seemed to go out of her, and she sank onto the edge of the cot.

"Won't you sit down, Mr. Thurston?" she asked uncertainly.

"Thank you, ma'am."

Jeff didn't understand. It had happened too fast. But he did want one thing put straight. "It hurt like Holy Ned when the doctor put my collarbone back in place," he said gruffly.

They sat there a moment, all groping for some way to pick up the talk. Impulsively, the schoolmaster burst out.

"I'll wager you didn't get all F's when you were in school, did you, Miss Becky?"

"Don't let him start asking questions," Jeff advised meanly. "You've got to ask him ones instead. Hard ones. He likes that."

"Score two, Jeff," Thurston said agreeably.

"You're a strange one!" Becky laughed in a curious, flustered way. For some reason, she wasn't angry at all any more. "No wonder the town can't decide about you, sir."

The teacher took this seriously. "They can't? Then they should try harder. They're letting me teach their children—the most delicate and important task one person can delegate to another. If they don't know what sort of man I am, they should not just question me—they should cross-examine me without mercy until they are satisfied."

"Do it, Becky!" urged Jeff. "Ask him tough ones!"

"Yes, ma'am. Do it!" Thurston stood up, put his hands behind him as if he were called on to recite, and waited expectantly.

"Oh lawsy, sit down, sir!" She smiled.

"It's more stimulating to thought, to stand on one's feet. That's why I insist that my pupils stand to give their lessons." The teacher seemed entirely earnest. "Go ahead, Miss Becky. Shall I help you start off? Where am I from? St. Louis, Missouri. How long have I been teaching? Six years. Where have I taught before? In Illinois and Missouri. Where did I receive my own education? At Washington University, in St. Louis. Were my grades good? Tolerably—I didn't do too well in French, never liked those irregular verbs." He paused and waited hopefully for her to go on from there.

Becky regarded him with a little speculation. "I've no child to be taught by you, but if I did I'd ask you one thing: Why did you come to Bearcat?"

Thurston tipped his head back and considered that a few seconds. Then his look leveled with hers. "That's a question with a number of answers. One of the reasons I came here was that there was important work to do. Another factor, of course, was that so many people opposed it so bitterly." He smiled a little and would have gone on, but they were interrupted by the sound of the back door slamming.

Harry Danver came in through the kitchen. He looked surprised to find the schoolmaster there, but more than that he looked riled about something—as

98

mad as Jeff had ever seen him. The clench of his teeth showed between his lips and he was pale.

Becky started up, alarmed. "Pa, what's wrong?"

Danver didn't speak—he stood there looking at their visitor. Thurston seemed to understand and made a move toward the door.

"Well, I'll take my leave of you—"

But Danver said, "Not yet. Not unless you want to, I mean."

The teacher hesitated, waiting while Pa still stared him up and down, sharp enough to bore holes.

Finally, Danver went on slowly. "There's something happened that you're going to learn of anyhow. Some of the fellows are already on their way to look for you. Seems like we need somebody to try to make sense out of things, talk straight to us so we can think straight. Deacon just keeps on saying we got to sit tight. Me, I don't know. I wish I was sure where you stand."

"I stand on my own opinions," Thurston said steadily. "They may not always be right, but I stand on what I believe. And I believe there'd have been no progress in the world from the beginning of time if men had always sat tight. It may be the way to avoid a conflict, but it ruins a man's self-respect to sit with folded hands when action is called for."

"That sounds all right," Danver agreed, "but a man can learn to talk fine and not mean it. How can we know for certain whose side you're on?"

Slowly the teacher answered, "I wasn't on any side. I didn't feel I had the right to be, because I haven't lived

99

among you long enough. But then Pete Regan dealt me into the game. Doesn't that establish my position better than words?"

"Them men was masked," Pa reminded him. "How do you know they were Regan's men?"

"The orders they gave me—to get out of town—could only have come from someone who considers himself in authority. They specifically accused me of 'stirring things up.' And that, I plead guilty to. I've tried to stir up the minds of my pupils, and, like making ripples in the center of a pool, that sort of stirring spreads out in all directions. If men start using their heads, who but a petty dictator like Regan would object?"

"He could have just fired you."

"He doesn't want to fire me—he wants to make me run," Thurston said thoughtfully. "He wants the town to see me turn tail, so that if they have put any trust in me, it will be destroyed."

"Regan ain't that smart," Pa stated positively.

"Possibly he's had instructions from higher up. I don't know much about the Company," Thurston said. "I was hired by an Eastern lawyer and haven't spoken a dozen words with Regan himself since I came. I don't know who has recognized me as a possible danger—presumably someone who sees that it may cost the Company money if the miners start to stand on their human rights. Someone doesn't want the men to develop independence."

And there the talk stuck. They stood silent, the two men and the girl, in a room swarming with unspoken doubts. Jeff felt left out. As usual, they'd gone on talking and forgotten he was there. He wished he could really shock them—jolt them into noticing. And it occurred to him that there was a way—that it would serve to make Ben Thurston eat those dirty words about needing to learn common sense and being a tomfool and all.

"Ben," he said, almost patronizingly, "did you tell anybody in town about the chain?"

They all looked at him, startled.

Thurston shook his head. "I told no one but you."

"What chain?" Pa asked.

"I believe he's referring to the fact that my attackers used a piece of chain on me," Thurston explained, but he looked puzzled.

It did Jeff more good than iron tonic to be able to put Thurston in his debt and do it with his wits, too. Coolly, he explained.

"Well, then, I guess the only other ones who could have known would be the men who jumped you. And Sammy Yates knew." Jeff could have crowed at the dumfounded looks on their faces. "He gave it away that day when we were going down into the mine."

Ben Thurston began to smile. *Score three for you* —it was written all over his face. Jeff had to admit that at least the teacher knew when he'd been bettered.

Harry Danver was slower to take hold of the news, but when he did make up his mind, it set like concrete. "That's good enough for me," he said, and stuck out his hand to the teacher.

"But what was your news, Pa?" Becky reminded him.

"Just this: Sammy Yates is back in town," he said. "He's been made timekeeper; they shoved out poor old Yankowitz, after him being timekeeper seventeen years. What's more, Sammy's been made deputy sheriff. He's packing two Colt .45's."

10

*N*ine days passed before the whistle blew for work, and when it did the miners went up the hill. Bitter quiet they were, but they went. Left below, the women watched—uncertain and worried, wanting to protest and to help their men protest, but . . .

"Who dares to question the right or wrong of things when Pete Regan knows every cent that's owed at the Company store?" Becky said it with that new angry flare in her eyes. "It was probably Regan who told McNish to ask us all for part payment on our bills, right now when there's been no work for days."

Quiet as she always was, Becky had suddenly taken

to talking like this to Jeff—not to anyone else. When the others were around she just held her peace, with a faraway look on her young sensitive face. Now that the two of them were alone in the kitchen, she let loose as if it had been bottling up inside her all morning.

"Even with the men going back to work today, payday is still two weeks off. Everybody will have to ask the Company for scrip, to pay their bills now, and Regan knows it! And scrip has just gone down—now it's only worth seventy-five cents on the dollar. It's not right!"

Jeff, still fretting under the leisurely life enforced by his mending bones, sat back gingerly in a kitchen chair and regarded his sister judiciously.

"You sound like Ben Thurston," he remarked.

The schoolmaster had been coming over regularly these past few nights, to talk to little groups of miners who drifted in quietly. Nobody else dared offer the men a place to meet, but Harry Danver had allowed that a man has the right to ask his friends in if he wants. And almost always Becky lingered somewhere near, to listen. After the others left, she always had an extra cup of tea made for the teacher—Jeff had noticed that, too. Now it dawned on him that she had even picked up a good deal of the schoolmaster's talk—too much to be fitting for a girl.

"You'd best leave the mine and things like that for men to figure out," he told her with some superiority.

"Nonsense! It's the women who have to make ends

meet, raise their children on a few cents a day and watch their menfolk go down into the hole, never sure whether they'll come back up again." Becky lowered her voice in a hushed tone of confidence. "When the accident bell rang, up at the powerhouse that day, we all heard it. And Ma knew—somehow she *knew* it was either you or Pa. The look in her eyes—!"

"Maybe you won't be marrying a miner." Jeff grinned. "Seems like you don't see all that trouble hanging around Ben Thurston's head any more."

She shot him a swift glance. "It's still there. I just understand it better."

Jeff didn't pursue it. He knew he shouldn't tease Becky—she'd been constantly good to him, this time he'd been laid up. Besides, it wasn't a minute later that Ma came bustling in the back door, herding the twins in front of her, all three of them mad enough to blow up.

"Deb in that corner, Dorrie in this one," their mother snapped, and the twin furies flounced off in opposite directions to take separate stands, face to the wall. The two identical calico-clad backs were rigid with injured feelings.

"What now?" Becky sighed.

Ma didn't answer, just motioned Becky toward the bedroom with a little tilt of her head.

As soon as the door closed on them, Jeff said, "Well, what mess did you get yourselves into?"

"We're not allowed to talk for a half-hour," whispered Dorrie hardly loud enough to hear.

Jeff went over closer. Knowing his mother's usual pick of punishments, he said, "You been talking out of turn again?"

"We did *not!*" whispered Deb so loud that Dorrie quivered.

"Be careful, Ma'll make it an hour!" she groaned.

Jeff chose Deb as the braver prospect and moved over to her side. "What happened?"

"It's so silly," she hissed. "We were just talking to the new clerk at McNish's. He's real nice—he gave us penny suckers. *Free.* So we were just being polite and Ma landed on us."

"Ma doesn't get sore over politeness," Jeff said suspiciously.

"Well, he just asked us a simple little question and so we just—told him."

"Besides," Dorrie muttered, "it was about you, so this is all your fault."

"What about me?" demanded Jeff.

"Nothing." Deb shrugged. "The man just asked if our pa was a miner, and we said our pa and our brother, too. We told him it was *our brother* caught the Company spy."

Jeff went back to sit down weakly at the kitchen table. He hadn't even been told there was a new clerk at the store, although the men did say that the town was getting more strangers day by day. Mrs. Stack's boardinghouse was cram-full, they said. That was another reason Thurston had told them to go back to work.

No—Jeff had to amend that—Thurston never told anybody to do anything. He just asked questions and the men had to come up with answers. Like last night. Thurston had said, "Regan knew why you walked off the job the day of the accident, but if you don't go back to work now, will he know why?"

"Regan don't give a hoot!"

"Of course he knows."

"Does he think we're gonna like that stool pigeon sittin' up there in the timekeeper's shack all soft, wearin' them shootin' irons where we can see 'em?"

"But is Yates the most serious complaint you have?" Thurston had gone on in that gentle, prodding way.

"No, certainly not. We're mostly worried about the timbering."

And another had said, "I'm mainly scared of all that dead air down there. Company ought to put in more ventilation."

"Me, I'm working in enough water to float a sail-boat."

So it went, with the miners coming to the conclusion that they had a lot of problems, but nobody had ever dared put the complaints up to Regan.

"First person to open their mouth would get fired so fast—!"

Thurston nodded. "It's not a one-man job, the way you've explained it to me. Your protest will have to proceed from all of you, and it may be you'll have to go over Regan's head with it. Meanwhile, if you haven't presented your case, what good will it do to stay off work?"

"Just give these drifters a chance to walk in and take our jobs."

Listening from his cot, where he was supposed to be asleep, Jeff hadn't been able to see that the talk solved anything. True, it helped sort out the miners' peeves into big ones and little ones, but what good did that do if they all just went on back to work, right past the desk where Sammy Yates sat triumphant?

Now, as Jeff sat pondering the whole business, his mother came back into the kitchen.

Glancing at the two culprits in their corners, she demanded, "Did they say anything?"

"Said they weren't allowed to talk for a half-hour," Jeff answered carelessly. And if it wasn't quite the whole truth, he thought it served her right for keeping such serious news from him. He was thinking he'd better start getting his strength back and find out what was going on around town.

"Reckon I'll go for a little walk, like Doc said," he remarked.

Ma looked worried. "Don't go far, and stay in sight of folks."

Making sure he had his slingshot, just for good measure, Jeff strolled up the street toward the Company store. It was fairly crowded with women, daring to stock up again on staples they had let run low during the layoff.

When they saw Jeff, they set up a big to-do. He'd forgotten that they would all make over him, the way women will. He tried to make himself inconspicuous, but the new clerk had already noticed him. A gray man in his forties—gun-metal hair and eyes like chipped ice—he wasn't tall nor small. A narrow, brittle-looking man, hard to pick out of a crowd and remember.

He didn't seem to pay any special attention to Jeff —he went on smiling in a humorless way as he handed out free candy to the younger kids. While Jeff stood there, surrounded by cooing females, he saw the clerk hand out a half-dozen lollipops. And McNish not ten feet away. The Scotchman didn't look happy, but he didn't say a word against it, either.

Working his way loose from the women, Jeff got out of the store. It was plain that this was no ordinary clerk—he didn't even look like one, and McNish didn't look like his boss.

As Jeff wandered on down the street, he was just as glad he'd brought his beany along. The new faces around town looked worse than the usual short-stakers, who were a seedy, shiftless lot but hardly dangerous. These men he saw now were tough—unshaven, dirty, almost rude the way they looked at the girls who strolled along the Row. The whole porch of Stack's boardinghouse was taken over by these bums—just sitting, whittling, waiting. For what? How did they all come to stop off here?

Jeff walked on slowly, his knees beginning to feel shivery. Turning down the railroad track, he reached the trestle over the creek and sat down in the middle of the bridge, letting his legs swing over the edge. Somehow he felt safer here, where he could see a good way in both directions, and above and beneath, too. The creek down there flowed gray and dirty with the sump water that the pumps fed into it out of the bottom of the mine, smelly dregs of seepage that had to be flushed out day and night, no matter whether the Bearcat worked or not. Only in some places, where the entries didn't drain, it collected. Jeff thought of standing knee-deep in it, hour after hour, swinging a pick. . . .

Instinctively, he started alert as someone came along the ties toward him. Then he saw it was just one of the Japanese section workers who maintained the tracks. The dark little man came up, walking soft-footed, but instead of going past, he stopped beside Jeff, the mysterious black eyes hidden deep behind the folds of his eyelids.

Softly, with an odd intonation, he said, "You come, please?" And he pointed down along the track. Where it cut through the low hill that separated the Row from Scotch Coulee there was a heavy growth of alder. "Man there, he say come. Very important."

"What man?"

"Man get off train. Stay down in woods. He say, friend."

Cautiously Jeff followed the Japanese. So seldom did

these silent, proud little people speak that he felt almost compelled to do as he was bidden. But as they neared the clump of woods, he stopped.

"I'm not coming any farther," he began—when he saw who it was, waiting just within the speckle of shadows. Hurrying forward, he shouted, "Tom Winkler!"

"Oh, my sainted aunt!" Winkler groaned. "It would be the dummy."

Jeff stopped within the shelter of the trees. Already the Japanese had gone off silently along the track.

Resentfully the boy retorted, "Dang it, Tom, don't be so sure. A lot's happened here since you left. I near got killed in the mine, tracking down the Company spy, the one that likely got you fired."

Winkler gave Jeff a second look. "We got word of an accident. It was you, you say?"

Quickly Jeff filled him in on the whole story. Tom listened silently, and when he spoke, it was in ordinary man-to-man tone.

"You go on home and tell your pa to meet me here tonight after supper. I got somewhat to tell him."

The moon was up, spreading its pale glow over the east while daylight still lingered in the west, as Jeff led his father to the spot where Tom Winkler waited. In the dusk, the two men shook hands.

Harry Danver looked at his son. "I reckon you'd better shy on back home."

It was just about the last straw to Jeff. He felt as if

bottom had been hit and busted through. Hopeless—just hopeless—to think that maybe they'd ever treat him like a human being. He was turning away, sick at heart, when he heard his father say something else.

"Hold up, son. I reckon you can stay." And to Winkler, he went on, "The boy may be backward in book-studying, but he's showed a good deal of gumption lately."

Jeff hadn't ever heard words that made him feel prouder. As they sat down beneath the trees, he eased onto a rock a little to one side, not wanting to press his luck.

"What brings you back, Tom?" Pa was asking. "You got trouble?"

"No trouble. Me and the family went over to Idaho —around Coeur d'Alene. I got a job right off. I'm making three bucks a day, don't have to buy from a company store and the mine's got to timber and ventilate good before we'll work. That's the rules. So when I got a week's layoff, Harry, I just had to come back and tell you how it is over there. You can pass it on to the men. I didn't want to come in town—it'd just start talk and maybe get you in trouble."

"How'd you know there's trouble going on around here?" Danver asked, surprised.

"It's all over the region how the Bearcat's brewing for a fight. Word's gone out from the Company that any goon who wants to come here is welcome. Every bum that can't get a job anywhere else is drifting up this way, waiting to snatch up the crumbs that get spilled."

Jeff swallowed dryly and his father looked grim.

"In fact," Tom went on, "the whole story about the cave-in has been put around, only not the truth. The way it came to us was that one of the miners rigged that rockfall to nail Sammy Yates. Yes, I know, Harry, the boy told me the real story this afternoon. So this is Regan's fairy tale, to make it sound like the miners' fault, and it's probably what he told the Company. There's even been a rumor that he's asked them to send in Pinkertons."

"What's—?"

"Detectives. That's how some of these companies have been keeping things under control. They plant Pinkerton detectives in town, to spy out any move that the men make toward organizing."

"That's what we've got to do—organize," admitted Danver, frowning. "We've got to get our signals straight so we all stand up at the same time to be counted."

"You're right!" Tom whispered sharply. "It's the only way you can ever deal with the Company. You have to lay down the law, say 'This is it, or else,' and if they don't listen to your grievances, if they fire just one man, then you all strike."

The strange new words hung on the air—Jeff wasn't even sure what kind of striking Tom meant, though he knew it wasn't outright blow for blow.

"I reckon that's about what we done the day of the cave-in," his father said. "We all went out, but now we're all back again. Schoolteacher said we better go back until we work out—like you were saying—just what our complaints are."

"Grievances. Don't ever call nothing a complaint. It doesn't sound good," Tom told him. "Trouble is, you all don't know how to go about this. What you need is to get help from the Federation, like the guys that helped Coeur d'Alene to organize. Came clear from Denver, told 'em how to set up work rules and how to picket, all of that. Oh, the Federation boys know a few tricks that the companies don't like, I tell you."

"What Federation?" Danver asked dubiously.

"Western Federation of Miners." Tom spoke the name low. "That's our union and it's spread all over the whole shebang—Idaho, Colorado, everywhere. That's what you need, big power."

"I dunno, I heard about unions," Danver said. "I heard they're full of radicals, what they call these anarchists."

"That's Company lies. The union is just a bunch of men like us, men that got tired of working for peanuts, with nothing to look forward to but getting shucked off when you're too old or crippled with rheumatiz, can't bust rock any more. So they did something about it. And they'll help you, too, if you ask 'em."

Abruptly Danver said, "Tom, come on home with me. You can't stay out here all night."

Winkler shook his head. "I'm heading over west

114

again right away. Besides, it wouldn't look good for you if somebody was to see me and guess why I came. It would mark you for chopping down, Harry. Because that's what Regan'll do if he catches you fooling around, organizing yourselves without knowing how. He'll chop down anybody that even looks like a leader. You need somebody outside the Company. So don't forget what I said—Federation will help you, they'll show you how to pull a good strike, with plenty of fireworks."

All the way home, Pa said not a word. Jeff, himself, was gripped by the excitement of what Tom had said, and more still by the firm way he'd said it. Just tell the Company it's got to cut out all this spy stuff—or else. Pinkertons—Jeff thought of the new clerk in McNish's store and shivered slightly. Marked to be chopped down—that was his own fate and he knew it.

As they came up the walk to the house, Jeff could make out that there was someone on the front porch. Pa stiffened, too. And then Becky called out to them.

"Evening, Pa—Jeff—"

There was somebody sitting there in the shadows with her; as they mounted the two steps to the porch, Jeff saw that it was Ben Thurston, who stood up and shook hands with Danver.

"Anything the matter?" Pa asked him nervously. "What did you want with me tonight?"

"Well, I—er—" the teacher sounded flustered for the first time since Jeff had known him— "I really just—

dropped by to—to pass the time of day—I mean evening —with Miss Becky."

It gave Jeff a secret enjoyment to watch the school-master flounder for once. Pa was relieved.

"Well, come on in, then," he said. "I got something to tell you."

Going straight on back to the kitchen, where there were lanterns lit and enough fire left in the stove to heat water for tea, the two men sat down at the table, while Becky got out the teapot. Jeff hung around the edges of the room, quiet and listening.

Danver went right through the whole of what Wink-ler had said, as if he'd been memorizing it all the way home.

Thurston listened thoughtfully.

"Well, what do you think?" Pa insisted.

"I'm not a miner," Ben answered slowly. "What do you think of it, Harry?"

"I've not made up my mind. But I know union has been tried back East. I've heard about these strikes. They had one in Ohio a few years ago, lot of shooting and heads broke, never did do any good. I know men that were in it—said the town dern near starved, finally had to go back to work on company terms."

"There are ways to do a thing—the right way, and all the other ways." Absently Thurston rubbed a hand along his neck where a few scars still showed. "I've heard something about the movement down in Colo-rado—this Western Federation has a pretty rough repu-tation. From what I hear, their way is to bully, to blow up or beat up or tear down a company until it gives in to the workers' demands. It seems to me that's as wrong as the companies' own brand of violence. Roughhouse shouldn't be necessary for men to settle their differences, even when men are forced to leave their jobs in a body to win their rights."

"I don't care much for rowdyin', either," agreed Danver. "But like Tom says, suppose it's the only way we get our—our grievements satisfied?"

As usual, Thurston came back with a counterquestion. "Has there ever been a representative of the Company come here to take a look at the mine operations —beside Regan, I mean?"

"Not since I been working the Bearcat, and that's fifteen years. Regan was here when I came, he's still here."

"And he must be drawing a handsome salary, to build a house like his and wear those rich clothes," the teacher mused. "The owners must be satisfied with his handling. It makes you wonder what sort of people we're all working for."

It gave Jeff an odd feeling to realize that he and Ben Thurston were working for the same outfit, hard to imagine that the Company, somewhere up above, resolved itself into actual human people. To think that somebody owned all of this—the very house and everybody in it! Some big unknown personage sitting far away in a mansion, with servants all over the place, carriages, probably two or three indoor privies. But there his imagination stopped short. He just couldn't picture all the details of such a far-flung notion.

Pa was evidently thinking the same sort of thoughts. As if from some back part of his mind that spoke without his leave, he said, "I never felt like I was working for a living soul. You're just chained to a big wheel that hauls you up the hill in the morning and lets go of you at quitting time, but only far enough to dangle back home a while. It's got no name or face, and Pete Regan just turns the power off and on."

Thurston looked up with a quick spurt of appreciation. "You've put your finger on it, Harry. The job you do isn't a man-to-man trade of work for pay any more. You've got too little to say in the deal. You need to get back some feeling of contact. A handshake takes two men's hands."

Pa laughed mirthlessly. "Regan would just as soon see you dead as dirty his hands on yours."

"Then we've got to get beyond Regan."

"How? Send somebody to Butte, where the head office is? Tell him to walk right in and give the big shots what-for? Ben, you know dern well a miner wouldn't get past the front door."

"Maybe not. But a committee might—a whole committee elected by the body of miners, your constituted representatives. How could the Company dare turn you down?"

"You go holding an election around here and Regan will unhire every man of that committee so quick—!"

"What's your solution, then?" the teacher asked, frowning. "Appeal to Denver as Winkler suggested?

That's as remote as Butte. And once an outside body of organizers gets in here, how can you control them? If they start slashing and dynamiting, do you think you'll ever really get a clean working relationship with the Company?"

Danver shook his head. "Lord knows I don't hanker for anybody to get hurt. I don't like the idea of calling in outsiders any more than you do—we already got too far out of the habit of handling our own selves. Wouldn't set good with me to have somebody from outside come tell us how to do our organizing. Least-ways not if we can do it ourselves. You reckon we can?"

"I'd say you can do anything if you want to badly enough," Thurston said soberly. "And if you do it, it'll be done just the way you want it done. Look, suppose I call a meeting at the schoolhouse—just a friendly get-together for parents to come and talk to the teacher about their youngsters, plus any other problems they might have? Could you make sure the men come, and know why they're coming, without Regan finding out?

Pa was nodding as the idea worked on him.

"Once you're all there together," Thurston went on, "you could go to it fast. Sign a pact, committing you to stand together, then elect your chosen leaders and decide what your main requests are. I'll be glad to put your case in writing. And then you'll be on your way to a reasonable, peaceful settlement of your problems."

Danver grinned at him dryly. "You make it sound almighty easy, Ben."

11

*T*he single large classroom of the schoolhouse was lighted up like a birthday cake. It smelled like one, too, what with all the cookery the ladies brought. It wouldn't be a "sociable" if they couldn't bake for it, each one trying to outdo the next, all the while putting on smiles and telling each other that their recipes really weren't hard—nothing to it! With so much talkety-talk, they more than made up for the absence of the men, who had idled on down to the cloakroom at the back of the building.

There was barely enough room for Jeff to edge into the close little windowless chamber without squeezing his tender ribs too severely. Thurston was in the center of the crowd of men, looking disheveled and hot. He was reading aloud, in a low, clear voice, the simple articles that all of them were to sign, binding them together in agreement; Harry Danver was passing out bits of paper to each of them for the voting.

When Thurston had finished, questions flew thick and fast.

"How many names do we put down?"

"How's the vote gonna be counted?"

"O.K. if we put your name in the pot, teacher?"

Ben shook his head. "It wouldn't be right for you to be represented by anyone but a member of your own calling. This has to be your play. I'll help all I can, but I can't be one of your union."

"Oh, dear," moaned the Deacon. "I don't like that word 'union.'"

"It's a good word, sir," Thurston said strongly. "It's part of the history of this country—it appears on some of the great flags that have flown over our states. It's a word linked with liberty."

"That's different," the Deacon argued. "Liberty is all right and so is a union of states, but this—this secret making of compacts. Oh, my friends, the Good Book says it's a sin to join together in any covenant except the true brotherhood of holiness."

It made some of the men hesitate—a little spell of doubt fell on the room. Thurston frowned.

"Where does it say that in the Bible, Deacon? I don't recall it."

"Time after time." The pudgy little man rolled his

eyes. "It tells about brotherhood in too many places to mention them all. It says, too, that it's not for the lowly to walk into the temples of the mighty."

"I'm no expert on Scripture," Thurston said, "but I do recall a line from Proverbs: The rich and poor meet together—the Lord is the maker of them all."

"Dern tootin'," said Harry Danver, and that was that.

As the voting went forward, Jeff wrote three names on his ballot, as they were all instructed to do, and dropped it into the cigar box. Feeling a little stifled, he edged out of the crush of men and cracked the door to get a little air. What he saw out in the classroom gave him a jolt. Coming in at the front of the building was the gray man, McNish's new clerk.

"Spy!" he hissed.

As the others went stiff, Thurston shoved through the crowd and came to look. "Oh, yes. The storekeeper who gives away candy."

"Let's get out of here," quavered one of the miners, all in a panic. "Is that back door unlocked?"

"Shut up your coward talk!" Harry Danver ordered roughly. "You gonna pile out of here like a bucket of minnows let loose?"

"It's all right," Thurston murmured. "The ladies are taking care of him for the moment. Let's finish the balloting—we may have to save the grievances for a further meeting." To Jeff he added, "If you've already voted, it would be good if you'd go out there and keep your ears open."

Jeff went, not knowing whether to feel compli-

mented or whether this was a dirty teacherish trick of
the schoolmaster's to get him out of harm's way.
Though what the gray man might do—? Draw a gun
and shoot them all down? Throw a bomb?

A half-dozen of the women had closed in around
the man and were giving him a vocal welcome that
would have drowned him if words had been water. All
the while he was answering up politely, the cold, color-
less eyes were searching the room.

His name, he said, was Mark Morse. Yes, he had a
family—wife and two girls—whom he intended to bring
here soon, which is why he'd thought to attend the
parents' meeting tonight. But when they asked him
what the girls' names were, he had to fumble.

Still scanning the room, he remarked, "I didn't know
this was a gathering for ladies only. And where is the
schoolmaster?" The question had an edge like a thin
knife under a piece of silk.

"Well now, you know how men are," chattered one
of the women. "They have to have their man-talk."

"School business, natcherly," added another sturdy
goodwife.

A third said, tittering, "They think all we're useful
for is to cook. My land, you must be lonesome for a
bite of home bakin'. Won't you sample my coffee-
cake?"

Jeff marveled at how expert they were at it. The way
they smiled and drew Morse over to the table where
the delicacies were laid out, it was enough to make
you never trust a woman again. There wasn't a one of

them who hadn't instructed her small fry they'd get
tanned good if they so much as said "howdy" to Mc-
Nish's clerk, yet here they were, themselves, acting as
if he were the guest of honor. Even Ma was giving
him some of her divinity fudge.

Morse let them delay him awhile, but Jeff could see
he was a purposeful man.

"If your good husbands are in a meeting, I'd like to
join them," he insisted. "I've met you kind ladies in the
store, but I've not had the pleasure of getting ac-
quainted with your menfolk." And he was actually
working his way toward the door of the cloakroom
when he found himself confronted by Becky Danver.

"Lawsy, sir," she said firmly, "the men are in there,
of course. But don't you know, they'd not take it
kindly to have a stranger come in on them while they're
discussing the private problems of their children.
You've got to live here a while before you can join in
a thing like that."

It was said so simply, it seemed to take Morse back
a pace. And it was so much the truth, he couldn't override her or skirt around her without seeming rude. For
a minute, he stood looking hard at Becky.

"If you'll pardon the observation, Miss," he said
coolly, "you remind me of someone—" And happening
to glance at Jeff, he nodded. "There's the lad, now. You
two bear a strong resemblance."

"He's my brother," she said, without a tremor.

Jeff sank, inwardly. Because it was plain, from the

124

way Morse gave a little smile and a bow, that the whole Danver family was being marked for chopping down.

It wasn't long until the men came out, sober and innocent, to mingle with the ladies. Some gave Morse a cool nod; others, not even that. The room was hushed as they all began to eat their refreshments—just the opposite to all the giddy small talk of a minute ago. Even the womenfolk kept still now.

Morse was no man to be frozen out easily, though. Stepping up to confront Ben Thurston, he eyed the teacher boldly.

"I've heard a lot about you, schoolmaster," he remarked. "Heard you've got some interesting teaching methods. If I'm going to bring my kids to this town, I figure I ought to know how the school's run, eh?"

"Absolutely," Thurston agreed. "Anything you'd like to know, sir, I'll try to tell you."

"Well, just what do you teach, schoolmaster? Do you teach reading, writing, and arithmetic? Or do you get off onto subjects that maybe don't belong in a classroom?"

Everybody was fairly scandalized that he would put such a suspicious question so bluntly to the teacher. They waited for Thurston to make an evasive answer, but Ben's face was beginning to take on a look that Jeff recognized—a willingness, even anticipation, to grapple with his questioner.

"Suppose," the teacher suggested, "that I put on a

demonstration of my classroom method—that is, if everybody is agreeable?" He glanced around, as the others nodded uncertainly. Jeff was just settling down to enjoy this, no matter who won, when he suddenly found himself thrust right into the middle of it.

"This young man"—Thurston was beckoning to him —"is of the age to enter eighth grade, so I'll ask him to play pupil while I set out an ordinary eighth-grade problem. Will you go to the board, Jeff?"

Thunderstruck, the boy walked forward, all eyes turned on him. Inside, he was rigid in the grip of conflicting emotions. Of course he had wanted to prove to them all that he really was no dummy, but to do it a man's way—not at a blackboard, on Ben Thurston's terms. It reminded him of all the times he'd stood defiant and refused to make even the first move toward solving problems, while the gang looked on, grinning. But the gang wasn't here now, the gang didn't matter. What counted was the desperate little play that was going on under the steely stare of a Company detective. Jeff knew that if he pursued his private war with Thurston, he might ruin a much bigger game—whatever it was—and, looking up at that quizzical, scholarly face, Jeff saw an intentness there that meant the stakes were high. And yet, far back in Ben's eyes was a flicker of humor, too, that was just for Jeff and no one else. *Either be a dummy or show yourself up as a fake.* The trap was perfect—he was daring Jeff to find a way out.

"This will be an arithmetic problem," Thurston began in his most punctilious manner. "We'll start with two imaginary mining companies—call them A and B. Will you head up two columns, please?"

Unhappily Jeff did as he was told, taking pains to keep his handwriting neat and legible. It nearly broke his heart to let Thurston win this way.

"Now," went on the teacher, "Company A hires seventy-five pick-and-shovel workers at $3.00 a day, each digging $15.00 worth of coal a day. Find the company's gross profit first. Then we'll assume the company spends $200.00 a week on timbering and ventilation, plus other operating expenses which we will not consider here since they will be the same for both companies. Find the weekly net profit, please."

All the men and women were watching, wide-eyed and attentive, as Jeff converted the daily gross into weekly net profits.

"Now take Company B, Jeff. It pays its men only $2.00 a day, spends only $150.00 a week for timbering. Make that comparison of profit. It seems as though Company B would come out ahead. But here we get into another factor: In one week, ten men quit because of dissatisfaction, so deduct the amount of coal they would have dug. Now . . ." He was going so fast that Jeff had to scramble to keep up, rushing through the arithmetic more quickly than he would have believed he could possibly do it. "Now," Thurston was going on, "we'll deduct the cost of an accident—one small accident, where one day's output is lost by another ten men. Subtract, please—correct. Now we must revise the production figures for the rest of the men. We'll have

127

to assume they spend one hour of each day looking over their shoulders at that poor timbering, so figure one hour's time per man lost."

Dividing frantically, Jeff got the hourly output, multiplied by number of men, subtracted from total, converted into money loss, while the audience watched in taut attention.

"And," Thurston was rattling on, "we have to assume that Company B is upset over the lagging production and dissatisfaction among the men, so it must send in detectives. Let's suppose the cost of a snooper is—what? Anybody have an idea how much a private investigator costs these days? What's the going rate for a spy?" He turned and glanced out at the listeners.

Mark Morse looked to one side and to the other, as if measuring the solidarity of the group around him. Shrugging, he said to Thurston, "You've put on a good demonstration, teacher. No need to carry it further. I'm convinced that you at least know how to exercise a pupil's mind—in fact, the boy looks quite warm." Without bothering to go through the motions of leave-taking, Morse strolled toward the door.

The minute he was outside, the men closed in around Thurston grinning.

"You called his hand!"

"Right to his face, you laid it on the line."

"That'll teach him we're no fools, to be cozied along—"

Jeff was hemmed in, elbow to elbow with the school-master. He couldn't get away, and yet he couldn't stand the look on his father's face, as Danver stood staring at him.

"Harry," somebody said, chuckling, "I thought you told us your kid was back'ard?"

"I never seen faster calculatin' in my life."

"Me, I couldn't have done them sums for love nor money."

But Pa just stood there hurt. There was no triumph in him as he said, "The boy must have been foolin' me all these years. And if there's one thing worse than bein' dumb, it's playin' dumb." He looked at the schoolmaster, blinking. "I'm all mixed up."

Now that the tension of conflict was over, Thurston seemed deflated and weary. He shook his head. "Don't blame Jeff. Maybe he belonged in the eighth grade all the time. Or maybe there never before was a good enough reason for doing arithmetic. A teacher should know how to handle these things. If you want to blame somebody, blame me."

To have Thurston try to cover for him just made Jeff squirm all the more.

Bitterly, he said in a low voice, "Score ten dozen for you, Ben, and I hope you choke on 'em."

12

*N*o one was supposed to know who the committee members were—no one but Thurston and the men themselves. Not even their families were to be let in on it. For greatest safety, the miners had agreed to entrust the counting of the ballots to the schoolmaster. He was to alert the six men elected, get them together for the necessary meetings, and draw up papers to present to the owners of the mine, stating their case and setting forth grievances.

Meanwhile, the rest of the town seemed to go on in the same drab routine of daily life, but that was only the surface look of things. Underneath, the sense of acceleration was there, as hot as if a deep vein of coal had caught fire underground. And if a few sparks erupted once in a while, that was only natural.

One of the miners would lash out at some mean-faced drifter who had got too nosy—fists would fly for a minute, and the punk would land sprawled on the ground. Or maybe a voice would strike up a cocky work song as the men came down the hill at quitting time, just a touch of smartness in their stride as they stepped to it:

"*In eighteen hundred and eighty-two,*
I traded the old world for the new. . . ."

Harry Danver said there was more coal being dug than he'd ever seen dug before—not that the men wanted to, but they had to burn off their energies some-how. They could even talk of the old Bearcat with a certain affection, since it was giving them partnership in each other. If you weren't in the mine these days, you weren't in their spirits or their thoughts.

Jeff almost wished he could go back to work. Even though he had just about recovered from his injuries, Big Stan wouldn't take him back into the tipple until he could turn the scales at 135 pounds. Being a good way short of that didn't really sadden Jeff, but on the other hand it left him restless.

The gang had come around, those days when he had been convalescing. They had admitted that Freck wasn't half the catcher that Jeff was; they'd even begged him to come back and help coach the team, if nothing else. But he had no stomach for baseball, and their second-guess friendship sat a little sour.

In fact, Jeff felt like a stranger to the whole world, even to his own family. It was a lonely sensation—it made him hold still inside, trying to hear some instinct that would tell him where he belonged, even as the town too was trying to listen to its own pulse.

"This union idea is a big thing. Ben says it's springing up all over the country, so big it could get pretty rough if it's not handled careful." Pa puffed his pipe as he held forth, to no one in particular. "Just like Ben says, it's got to be lawful, but we got to show 'em we mean business, too."

It was a rainy Sunday two weeks after the union charter had been signed in the schoolhouse. The kitchen of the Danver home was steamy and comfortable with the smell of the gooseberry jam that Ma was putting up. Pa was easy off, feet cocked on the coal bucket beside the stove. He'd been snug as a cat lately but trying not to show it. Putting that together with his new mysterious way of taking a late walk every other evening or so, it was plain, to Jeff at least, that his father had been elected a committeeman.

Ma and Becky sensed it, too. When Jeff looked at his sister, he saw awareness in her face; when Ben Thurston was mentioned, it flamed up bright. Even now as she sat quiet by the rain-struck window, cradling the baby in her lap, Jeff could see something quicken in her eyes at Pa's words—some of that fox fire.

Ma wasn't so sure—not sure about anything. "I know

Mr. Thurston's smart and all, but—" She frowned as she skimmed the jam.

"Smart! He writes out them forty-dollar words quick as a city lawyer. You ought to see how—" Danver checked himself, on the verge of giving away his big secret.

Ma stuck to her doubts. "Well, I never did hold with lawyers and I don't know if I hold with him. Oh, he talks good enough; he could talk a bird out of a tree. But I can't help thinking, why's he doing all this for us?"

"Ma, you ain't built for thinking," Danver told her, not unkindly. "I got this all figured, so don't fret your head. Ben's mad on account of being beat up, and this is how he's gonna get even with the Company. It's that simple."

"Oh, Pa!" Becky murmured a protest in spite of herself.

Danver looked over at her. " 'Oh, Pa' what?"

"Ben's not like that. He's not doing this out of some spite."

"Oh, so you're an authority on Ben these days," he teased.

"Well, I know him well enough to know he's not a small-minded person," she retorted. "He's the kind who's got to stand up and speak against anything unjust. He's a—an *opposite* kind of man. When a thing seems impossible to tackle, he's got to tackle it."

"That's what I mistrust," Ma said plaintively. "Why would a body want to mix into other folks' troubles,

133

when they're so almighty hard to fix up?"

"It's because he's got imagination," Becky tried to explain. "He takes any kind of unfairness very hard —he's just built that way." She had a wonderful shine in her face. "He's the kindest, gentlest man. . . ."

"Beck-y loves Ben, Beck-y loves Ben, haaa-haaa-haaa!" Fiendish twin squeals of mockery issued from behind the door to the bedroom.

Ma started; Pa scowled. Becky blushed and Jeff didn't even feel sorry for her. Calling Ben Thurston "kind" and "gentle"—!

"If you ask me," he remarked, "Thurston's mixing into this because he's always itching for some kind of fight."

"Can't recall asking you." Pa chewed the pipe hard. He still hadn't forgiven Jeff for the turn of events at the schoolhouse. Harry Danver was a slow man to get over a thing, especially when he felt he'd been shown up as a fool. The other men hadn't helped, either. They'd been rawhiding him unmercifully about not knowing he'd fathered a "boy wonder"—a real humdinger of a genius! Oh, they'd poured it on strong for a while.

Having the talk swing to the other extreme was no more joy to Jeff than being thought stupid, and just as untrue. But he couldn't seem to get to his father, to speak to him about it. There was a breech between them which had been summed up in Pa's bluntest way:

"I'm glad you ain't dumb," he'd said, after it was all over that night, "but I'm danged if I understand it. All

I know is, them F's on your report card weren't Ben Thurston's fault." And leaving the rest of that humiliating thought unspoken, he had shut himself off from Jeff, to where the boy sometimes wondered if they would ever again be as near as they were once, coming up the slope of the mine in the darkness, drawn along wordlessly close together. . . .

Now as he sat squelched, on a hard chair half hidden behind the stove, Jeff subsided gloomily, hoping that somebody would feel a little sympathy for him. But their thoughts were all focused ahead, with this quickening pace, this tempo that you either ran with, or bolted away from.

Ma set a pan down on the stove top with a sharp clatter. "Harry, I wisht you'd get out of this!"

Danver glanced anxiously toward the bedroom door. "Don't know what you're talking about."

Becky gathered the sleeping child into her arms and went off to the next room. They could hear her chiding the twins softly. "Haven't you anything better to do than snoop? Where's your darning, Dorrie? Deb, those shoes need polish. Right now!" The door closed behind her.

Ma turned again and faced her husband, nervous but determined. "Suppose you get in trouble?"

"I won't get in any trouble," he told her in a low voice, "unless this family gets me into it! Good grief, woman, don't you know by now that pair in there have ears sharper than a splinter? And they talk near as much as their ma does."

135

She wouldn't be put off, though. "They like to eat, too. What if you get fired? We owe near a hundred dollars to McNish."

"Instead of thinking like that," Danver told her, "why don't you concentrate on how nice it'll be to have a whole extra dollar, maybe, for every working day? You could buy you a new dress, get one of those velvet pillow-covers with the pictures on it that you've been wanting—"

"Well, that'll be fine if it ever happens," she said without enthusiasm, "but I still say why does it have to be you? Why can't somebody else do the meetin' and talkin'?"

"I should let another man stick his neck out for me?" Pa scowled at her angrily.

"Well, I mean, somebody without kids—"

"Kids? Kids weren't put on earth to keep a man knuckled down. Took me a long time to figure this, Ma, and I got her figured good. The kids need a pa that won't back off when he's called on to head up a good fair thing that needs doing. Thurston says right when he says nothing ever got made better by sitting still."

"Oh, I swear, Ben Thurston's got you up in the clouds!"

"What of it?" Danver stood up, his lanky, wire-hard body uncoiling out of the chair like a spring. "It's better'n being sunk in a hole, with no hope except to hope the mine don't fall on you. Don't try to undo me, Ma. Thurston is the first man ever bothered to talk to me that made sense. I been listening to him quite a spell now; I trust him. If that turns out to be wrong, then I'm dumb. I'm so dumb, I'd just as soon pull the hole in after me!'"

As Jeff stood alone on the front porch that evening, those words came back to him. He understood that feeling, of needing to prove himself or else crawl away into some hole. But he had never thought that a person as old as his father could still feel unsettled. He'd always taken for granted that when you grew up, you just naturally knew that you were right. About everything.

At least a man should. Women were born fearful—that, he realized. As Jeff stood there with the slackening drizzle still falling lightly, speckling his face, a sudden coolness came over him—to think that right this minute he was steadier than Ma. Becky was different—he wasn't sure why. She was calm, herself, but she hadn't been able to quiet her mother's flutters this time, when Pa had gone off an hour ago on his nighttime stroll. Somehow they all had an inkling that this was the last, the important meeting where the papers would be signed. Then the only remaining move would be to present their case to the Company's head office in Butte.

So, all evening Ma had been jumpy as a horse in a lightning storm. She'd made mistakes in her knitting, she'd set the bread to rise without any salt in it, spanked the twins and then cried over them. Becky had tried to soothe her, but finally it was Jeff who had taken charge.

"It's time we were all in bed," he said. "You go along, I'll put out the lights." And Ma had gone, as meek as a kid. Becky had stayed with her, of course, to be near until Pa came home. Jeff had turned down the kerosene lamps, then stepped out on the porch to get a breath of air, the way his father always did before turning in.

Early August and the nights were already growing chilly. The keenness felt good, though—it had been warm in the living room this last hour. Out here it was quiet, too; most of the Row had settled down to sleep. A good time to think.

For the first time in his life, Jeff felt it was up to him to decide what to do—what he wanted to do. There had been a certain satisfaction in discovering that he could take the worst that Thurston could dish out, that night in the schoolroom. In fact, he thought if he chose to, he could go back and clean up on the class work, swallow down fast as much of it as he pleased. Then he might just get out of here, go wherever he liked. . . .

And yet, on the other hand, it took a tough man to bust coal. Mining was work you could take pride in, if you didn't have to crawl to Pete Regan. The dangers weren't so bad—breathing a little rock dust, or maybe carrying a canary in a cage to check for deadly gas—all this you could take if there wasn't too much of it. But to feel that you were personally an earthworm to the mine boss, to be squashed at his pleasure—that was the bad part. So, maybe that was on the way out. Maybe tonight was going to be the beginning of the end of that.

Standing there in the wool-cloudy dark, his hand resting carelessly on the lintel of the porch roof overhead, Jeff realized with a stroke of inner perception that he could take hold of the beam with all five fingers, whereas a couple of months earlier he could barely reach it with his middle finger by stretching. . . .

And at that instant the night split apart! A roar, a blazing tower of flame shot up—the blacked-out houses were highlighted in a red glare. Somebody screeched.

"Fire! Fire!"

Jeff was down off the porch, running for the end of the Row, where flames streamed and flowed up the sides of one of the buildings—the cardhouse. Always closed on Sundays, nobody supposed to be in there, how could it have started? Even as he pounded down the street, Jeff had a terrible fear of what the answer was. People were coming out of their houses, half undressed, running as they buttoned themselves up—

And there ahead, they saw the front door of the cardhouse burst open, and six men piled out into the weird devilish light, stumbling to get shut of the building which was already a furnace. Jeff rushed to his father.

"Are you hurt?"

Danver shook his head, dazed, brushing crumbs of fire from his clothes. The other committeemen stood shaken, staring up at the fiery death they had so narrowly escaped. Frightened townspeople were starting to close in around them, then fell back as if at a stroke.

Pete Regan had walked onto the scene. At his elbow was Sammy Yates, fingering the pearl handles of those two Colts. Against the muteness of the crowd, the flames made a fierce crackle. They made a shifting glare across the stricken faces that ringed the spot in the street where six men and a boy stood alone, like untouchables.

Regan smiled. It was a terrible grimace for that heavy-set face, the smile of a killer bull. From under the black Stetson, he eyed the committeemen, his feet set square, fists dug into his beefy flanks.

To Sammy he said, "Ask 'em what they were doing in there."

Strutting forward a step, Yates demanded loudly, "All right, speak up fast. What was you doin' in there?"

"What are you doing here, Sammy?" Harry Danver snapped back. "How'd you get here so fast? You're all dressed like for a picnic in the park. Could it be you was expecting this to happen? Maybe you got a match or two on you?" His voice rose with the kind of fury that breaks loose in a moment of defeat. Speaking across Sammy, he was challenging Regan, too. Jeff held his breath. It had never dawned on him that his father had this kind of courage.

"You talk big for a man that's one step from the jailhouse," Sammy informed him nastily. "You was breakin' the law, bein' in there, lettin' a fire get out of hand—you could've burned down the whole blame Row."

140

"Why should we set fire to the building we're in?" retorted Danver recklessly. "We near got killed. That was no hot-stove fire, it was set. I say it was set by somebody that wanted to flush us out of there—or kill us. Look how quick she burned."

And in fact, by now the cardhouse was just about done for, a caving blackened carcass. Men were on the roofs of the buildings to either side, pouring water on small patches of smolder, but the rain earlier that day had already wet things through and had probably saved the whole town from going up in smoke.

"Should I take 'em in, Mr. Regan?" Sammy offered willingly.

"Ask 'em what they were doing in there," Regan repeated. He hadn't stopped smiling.

"If a man wants to play a friendly game of cribbage," Danver shouted, "there's no United States law against that!"

"You better worry more what's the law in this town." Yates sneered. "You ain't answered the boss's question."

The mine boss was glancing around him at the crowd, his face crusted with scorn. "I'll tell you what they were doing, Sammy," he said in a gritty voice. "They were troublemaking. And they're not smart enough to be troublemakers. You got to have brains to make big trouble. When little peanut-heads try it, they end up out on a limb and don't even know why." He laughed. "Ask the rest of 'em"—he jerked a thumb at the crowd—"if anybody wants to step out in front and join up with these suckers. Maybe we should get out a piece of paper and write on it: *I am a sucker*, and let 'em all sign it."

The mocking words sent a shudder of mortification through the crowd like a draft of cold wind.

"Nobody seems to want all this-here brotherlyhood." Sammy snickered.

Regan nodded. "All the same, I'm holding the whole lot of 'em responsible. For the cost of this building, every man'll work the mine a day at no pay. And on account of them letting troublemakers get started, you can tell 'em if I see more than two men walking together, they'll be out of a job."

"What about those?" Sammy pointed to the six committeemen.

"They're fired. Tell 'em to pay up what they owe at the store and be out of town by tomorrow night, or go to jail for destroying Company property."

Yates stepped over to confront the crowd. "Well, you heard. You better git and git fast. You're breakin' the rules, bein' here right this minute."

Awkward, shamefaced, they shrank backward, less from Sammy than from the gleam of those eyes fixed on them from the shadow of Regan's Stetson. Nervously they separated, moved away from each other as if some contamination were spreading among them.

Harry Danver called out after them. "You ain't gonna let him pull this off? If we'd stick together, he couldn't—!"

But now Ma ran from the crowd to his side and threw her arms around him. "Oh, dear heaven! Don't get yourself sent to jail, Harry. What'll I do? What'll we all do?"

Under pressure of her frantic embrace, Danver slackened. Jeff could see the resistance ebb out of him, leaving him limp.

When the street was almost empty, Regan and Sammy turned away, strode back up toward the bench, leaving the committeemen and their families standing there, deserted.

Becky had come to put her arms around her mother comfortingly. "Pa," she whispered in a tortured voice, "where's Ben?"

"Yeah, Harry," said one of the others starkly. "Where's your pal, the schoolmaster? Why didn't he show up tonight?"

And a third miner called across. "What did Regan mean, we been took for suckers?"

Danver shook his head. "I dunno, but I'm going to find out. Right now."

It was a dejected little clutch of people who walked the length of the Row, past doors that were shut. They didn't talk. When they came abreast of the Danver house, Becky broke away from them to take her mother inside—Ma was crying hard now. But before they'd gone a hundred steps down the street, the girl came out again and hurried after them, carrying a lighted lantern. Her father didn't seem to notice.

Jeff thought Pa acted almost frozen—he hardly seemed to be taking things in. Not that there'd been much to see behind the burned building. They had found a few empty kerosene cans, nothing else. No doubt but that the fire had been set off deliberately; no way to tell who had done it.

Jeff ventured once to ask, "Who else knew about the meeting tonight?"

His father didn't seem to hear, but one of the other men answered. "Nobody knew but Thurston. When he didn't show up, we got worried. We checked around the table and none of us told a living soul."

And another added, "Looks to me like maybe we been flummoxed."

Becky made a little incoherent sound of ardent denial. "The way you've all been full of this, it must have slipped out without your knowing it. You can't really think, after all Ben's done to help, he'd turn now and hurt you?"

"Ain't a question of turning," muttered another of the miners. "He could have been on their side all along, just settin' us up like sittin' ducks."

Still Danver didn't speak, just led the way straight up the path to the unlighted cabin. Even before he knocked, the place gave off an empty feeling.

When no one answered, Danver thrust the door open —it wasn't locked. Taking the lantern from Becky, he held it high as they crowded into the single small room.

The place had been stripped bare of all but the

144

Company furnishings. The chipped dishes were washed and stacked on the shelves beside the stove, the cupboard was clean except for a few leftovers of tea and salt and crackers. In the closet, they found the bedding put away neatly; except for that, it was empty. The books were gone.

"Looks to me like he must have been planning this quite a while, to get all them books out of here without anybody noticing," remarked one of the men, discouraged. "Must have had to take 'em over to the depot at the county seat a box at a time, when nobody was looking."

"I don't believe it!" Becky burst out. "Ben's been tricked, too! Somehow he's been caught like the rest of you—they've taken him away, maybe they've hurt him or—" Her voice broke.

The miners shook their heads, unconvinced.

"Don't look like there's been a struggle."

"Body don't pack up everything if he's been kidnaped."

"Well, they did jump him once before," Jeff put in uneasily. He couldn't see why he should care so much what had happened to the schoolmaster, unless it was the deathly sick look that was coming to his father's face. Danver was pulling out the drawers of the desk, one by one. They were empty, too.

"I been thinking about that time he was roughed up," one of the miners was saying. "You know that could have been done by somebody besides Regan's bunch

—somebody maybe had a personal grudge."

"But Sammy Yates knew all about it—more than he should have," Jeff reminded them.

"Well, maybe that just goes to show. Maybe Ben and Sammy been good friends all through this."

"Oh, you can't believe such a thing!" Becky cried. "After the way he stood up to Mark Morse the other night?"

"Yeah, and nothing happened to him, neither. I wondered about that. After Thurston came out so blunt, I figured something cruel would fall on him, but nothing did."

"Probably all part of an act, to get us to trust him so's he could set it up for Regan to bust us good."

Jeff prowled out the back door—there was a drum out there that had been used to burn trash in. Something white showed, down in there—probably paper, he thought, couldn't see in the darkness. Before he could retrieve it and take a private look, his father had the same idea and came out in back with the lantern. The others grouped around as he plucked from the barrel a sheet of paper only partly smoked up, still readable.

On it were scribbled the words: "Here's the first five hundred. If you pull it off right, you'll get the rest of the money through the mail, as we agreed." It was signed by Pete Regan. There wasn't a man there who didn't know that black scrawl of his that signed the work orders—and the firing slips.

One of the men was digging deeper in the ashes; now

he brought up some crumpled sheets that hadn't quite burned—there was enough of them left to see that they were the union articles. Still visible at the bottom were some of the signatures of the miners.

"This don't prove—! It could have been planted." Harry Danver spoke harshly.

Then he broke off as he caught sight of something else—a fragment of paper that had escaped the barrel and come to rest under the doorstep. As he picked it up, they saw that it was covered with Thurston's own writing—Jeff recognized it better than most people, the angular script with the clean downstrokes and cross-strokes.

Frowning, Danver studied it—he wasn't much for reading, had to spell out anything like a big word. Finally he handed it to Becky.

"Read it out loud," he said.

In a tremulous, halting voice, she read, " '. . . happily, I have found that where men have grown to maturity without sufficient education or practice in the exercise of logical thinking, they are easily duped by anyone with a clever tongue and can be led to their own downfall. . . .' "

Jeff took the paper from her unresisting grasp—it had been torn after the word "downfall." He studied it, in the thin yellow light of the lantern, trying to put his finger on something wrong about it. And then he had it! To make the paper tear right at that word must have taken some careful manipulation; the same was true at the top of the fragment. Both edges were uneven, not torn straight across as paper always is when it's ripped carelessly.

"Pa—" he began. But when he looked up at his father, Jeff was stunned to silence.

Before their eyes, Harry Danver had got old and dull and beaten.

Part III

The Showdown

13

*T*he Deacon lived in a neat little house up behind the store. It had once been the postmaster's, until that elderly gentleman had retired a while back. Now the mail was handled at odd moments by the assistant bookkeeper of the mine, who had six kids and already had a big house. So when the Deacon had come to town, it was his good fortune—as he always said —to find the cottage unoccupied.

As Jeff knocked gingerly at the front door, he was shivering, and not just from the rainy chill in the morning air. He wondered why he should be nervous —it must be because everything was all hashed up. Everybody was acting petrified and looking over their shoulders at shadows. It had been this way for two days, since that ruinous Sunday night.

Seven more men had been fired on Monday, to convince the Row that Regan meant what he said when he'd instructed them to keep apart. The word from the mine was that Big Stan, Zack, and Willie Weber, the new stable boss, had their orders to keep a narrow eye on the men during working hours. Evenings, Sammy Yates strolled the town, flanked by two stubble-faced goons whom he'd appointed his assistants. All three carried sawed-off shotguns.

The result was that the whole town had put on a mask. The voices of the people were muffled; they even moved in a constricted way, as though natural rhythm had been cut off and living was only a stiff gesture.

The one thing that could still rouse a flicker of sensation in them was the mention of Ben Thurston. Not that his name was spoken—they simply muttered "him," and everyone knew who was meant. When Jeff had tried cautiously to talk about the schoolmaster, Pa had stopped him, in a low, toneless voice.

"If you ever say word-one about him around this house, it ain't your home no more."

Not that it would be home for any of them much longer. The Deacon had managed to get the ousted men a few days' suspended sentence. That Monday morning he had trotted around from this house to that, shaking his head, condoling and scolding and sighing. Finally he had gone up on the bench to confront Regan in person with a plea that the families be given more time. The mine manager had sourly granted them ten days to pack up—a small concession, but it did ease some of the worst pressure.

The Deacon had been the one pinpoint of color in these past gray days, so it was natural that Jeff should turn to him finally, after everyone else had made him shut up. He knocked again lightly, wondering if the Deacon wasn't maybe out somewhere right now, trying to shore up somebody's spirits. Just as he was about to turn away, though, the door opened and the pudgy little man looked out in evident surprise.

"Mercy, lad, you tapped so lightly I doubted my ears. Come in." He led the way into the parlor.

Jeff had heard about this room from other people in town. For being small, it was awesome—the walls painted dark, almost black, which was probably proper for a preacher, but not half so comfortable as ordinary blue or green. To one side there hung a big Bible painting with colors so strong they seemed to hover over you. And then Jeff discovered that the strange, uneasy light in the room was actually coming through odd-shaped pieces of celluloid laid over the inside of the window, sort of like stained glass, that let the sunlight through all tinted and checkered. It was just as uncomfortable as everybody said, though the Deacon had explained, at one time and another, how these "ascetic" surroundings were chastening to the spirit, so Jeff supposed it was all for his own good, to be allowed in here.

He was ushered over to one of the straight chairs which, except for the small pot-bellied stove in the corner, were the only furniture in the room.

"Sit down, my boy," said the Deacon, adding, "I myself never sit when engaged in the service of my fellow man. What can I do for you, child?"

It was nice of the Deacon to look at it that way, nice that he would want to be of service to just a kid, but Jeff wished he would sit down. The way he stood against that somber wall with the red and purple light from the window striking across his face, he seemed to be about ten feet tall and not quite human. It took all the purpose Jeff could squeeze together to speak out without sounding scared.

"I had to come," he began, "because my father won't listen to me—nobody will. And if they just would, they all might go back together. If they'd just do what Ben Thurston used to say, stand solid and not give in, I'll bet Regan would have to take back Pa and the others."

"Gracious, boy!" The Deacon looked amused, though he tried not to show it. "I'm afraid you're trying to grapple with some ideas that are beyond your simple scope."

"I'm not so simple," protested Jeff sorely. "Maybe I used to—act dumb sometimes, but I know what's going on. I know the reason the men all came to pieces is because they think Ben ran out on them."

The Deacon studied him, somewhat surprised. "I must admit that's a fairly good piece of reasoning, lad. Who prompted you to come here and say this to me?"

154

"Nobody!" Jeff wriggled on the hardness of the straight chair. It was warm in the small room; heat was coming from the stove. He wished he could stand up and walk around a little—Ben said you could think better—but the Deacon had cornered the privilege with all that talk about serving folks. So Jeff sat and tried to choose his words carefully, so as to be believed.

"I came because you've been helping everybody out, and I thought you'd want to know what I've found, so you can help them better. If you could talk them into not being mad at Ben, maybe they'd even organize up again, or write to the—the Federation, down in Denver."

The Deacon listened thoughtfully, his velvety dark eyes never leaving Jeff's. When at last he spoke, his voice was rich with kindness. "Poor child, someone must indeed have filled you with the ingredients of heartache. My son, you must know by now that rebellion can only bring sorrow and hurt. Haven't you already felt the full brunt of the downcast spirit in your own home? To suggest that this poor stricken community needs another spasm of hatred—this only reflects that your tender soul has been infected by half-truths, misunderstandings. I believe I'd better pray for you."

Jeff thought that if it was a matter of hatred, there was more of that around right now than there had ever been. "Thank you," he said doggedly, "only I still think they'd all feel better if they knew that Ben didn't turn on them. He's probably got himself killed for them." And to hear himself say the words aloud made

Jeff actually realize that it was likely true. It made him suddenly miss that irritating lanky villain of a schoolmaster acutely.

"What leads you to such a startling supposition?" the Deacon asked, frowning.

"Well, if he didn't turn coat, then he was probably marked for chopping down, along with Pa and the rest." Jeff had gone over it enough in his mind that the train of thought was loud and clear. "Ben always did say the Company would rather show him up in a bad light than just fire him. So I figure they must have done something with him, and then fixed things at the cabin to look as if he'd run out."

"You figured this? Yourself?" The Deacon looked skeptical.

"Yes, sir." Jeff nodded. "I had plenty of time to think. Nobody will talk to me—they aren't talking to anybody. They won't even let me show them the proof."

That interested the Deacon. "You have proof that Ben Thurston is innocent of this betrayal he's put upon us all? Tell me, lad, tell me! What proof do you have?" For once he sounded excited.

"This paper." Jeff got out that scrap of damaging evidence in Ben's own writing. "See how it's been torn just so? I don't know what else was maybe written, but somebody just picked out enough words to make it sound like Ben was tricking us. And I looked and looked through the trash barrel—there weren't any other scraps. Why would he just drop one piece where it would be seen? That's why I think it was put there on purpose, and the note from Regan, too."

The Deacon studied the bit of paper, shook his head. "I'm afraid your imagination is playing havoc with your small sense, lad. This is no proof that you have here. Who can tell why a man tore a piece of paper this way or that? As for the rest of this miserable piece of writing, he probably took pains to burn it. Sheer chance that this scrap escaped the fire, to convict him out of his own hand. Oh, the pity of it. . . ." Sorrowfully he headed for the stove with unmistakable intention.

Forgetting proprieties, Jeff lunged out of his chair and fished the bit of paper from the Deacon's fingers, much to the little man's astonishment. In fact, he was fairly peeved at being snatched from.

"Tut-tut, child." He frowned. "You're acting most strangely. I'm afraid you've been beset by some devil that's giving you an unruly spirit. The Good Book says that when devils seat themselves in some poor sufferer's soul, we must drive the fiends out with hard chastisement. I'm afraid I must speak with your father."

But Jeff was on eye level with him now, and the words didn't seem so mighty. In fact, he thought bitterly, the Deacon was just like the rest of them—so taken up with his own way of thinking he wouldn't listen to reason when it was shoved right under his nose.

Disappointed, wanting somehow to take a dig into that plump, positive little bundle of righteousness, Jeff spoke over his shoulder as he went out the door.

"That's all right, I'll get somebody to listen to me.

157

And I've got more proof at home, too—there were other things in that trash barrel."

It was a relief to get out into the air again, even if it was a damp, mizzly day. Across the dripping mountain slopes lay shreds of fog, and the high peaks were lost in rain clouds.

Discouraged, Jeff slogged on home. It was coming plainer all the time that he was the only one who wanted to pull things together. He wasn't even sure why he did want to, except that it had been a good feeling—a clean feeling—to think that someday he could maybe stand up to Pete Regan, like any other man, and give him back look for look.

When he got to the house, he avoided the kitchen, where the rest of the family drooped about the unhappy business of packing what few things they were to be allowed to keep—their clothes, the bed linens, but not a dish or stewpot, not even the ice-cream freezer. As usual, it was leaden quiet back there.

Noiselessly, Jeff slipped across the front room and climbed the ladder to the attic. Even in the middle, where the roof came to a peak, there wasn't room to stand straight, so he went on forward to his mattress on the floor and sat down to think.

In a cardboard box were the other bits of paper he had salvaged from the trash barrel when he'd gone through it carefully the morning after the fire. Burned, soaked with rain, these weren't really proof of anything, and Jeff knew it.

There was part of a list of grievances, written in

Thurston's hand, so he really had worked on the papers. But then, they'd just say that was part of his "act."

Another scrap—a page of a letter—seemed to be urging Thurston to come home. One sentence said, "When will you get over this stubborn fancy, Ben, and return to the life and people with whom you belong?" The rest of it was just family gossip, about a brother, about somebody called Uncle Cabot. Jeff wasn't even sure why he'd kept it, since it certainly didn't prove anything, either.

Finally there was a penciled draft of a letter, in Thurston's writing, addressed to a Mr. W. T. Emerson, Pres., Emerson Enterprises, Butte, Montana. It started out:

Dear Sir—
This letter is written in the belief that when a man has entered into a business where his profits are derived from the labors of other men, he has also entered into a responsibility toward those men. Granted that the individual worker has the theoretical right to leave your employ if it dissatisfies him, yet the economics of his situation may render him literally helpless to do so. And when the whole body of such workers unites to protest certain unfairnesses in their condition, a common decency demands that they be heard, in all seriousness.
Therefore, sir, we request . . .

That last word had been crossed out. ". . . urge that you grant us an appointment. . . ." The rest of the page was burned. Of course this, too, could be called a hoax, some gesture of Thurston's to make it look as though he were at work on the miners' problems.

And yet, putting them all together, Jeff was as sure as he had ever been of anything that the schoolmaster had been trapped as badly as the committeemen. Maybe worse.

Again Jeff read the beginning of the letter—such high-sounding words, it seemed a pity they would never be sent now. And treading on the heels of that thought came another. A peculiar impulse seized him, part anger, part wanting to get even with everybody—for his own sake—for his father's sake—even for Ben's. Delving into another box where he kept his belongings, Jeff dragged out his old school copybook and found a pencil.

Forming his letters as neatly as he could, with round tops and proper little tails at the end of each word, he copied the heading and the paragraph onto clean paper. Sitting back to admire it, he thought it was nearly as good a job as Thurston himself could have done, though the writing somehow didn't have quite the slash-and-cut of Ben's.

And then he found himself stumped. Never having written a letter before, Jeff hadn't the faintest idea how to go on. He wasn't even sure what he wanted to say. No point in asking for an appointment for a committee that was going to be dragging its tail out of town the first of next week. Maybe, he thought, the best thing would be just to put a nice ending on it and send it off —he was determined now to send it. But he didn't even know any endings.

He looked around absently, and there, staring him in the face from its place among his most valuable possessions—his slingshot, hunting knife, and shinny stick— was the book that Thurston had given him. It had sat there at his bedside all this time, not because of any usefulness, but in honor of its pure cash worth. A book utterly crammed with letters.

It gave Jeff a twinge of conscience now, to read the words Thurston had written inside the cover, although he knew he should not feel such sharp regret for the loss of someone who had been so aggravating. All the same, with Ben gone and probably done for, Jeff had no heart to hold onto the old grudge.

Thumbing through the pages, he saw that he'd come to the right source for fancy endings. In one place, he noticed that there was a good deal of underscoring in pen. It was a letter from Thomas Jefferson to James Madison, all about government. Jeff turned the next page and saw more pen lines under the words ". . . Educate and inform the whole mass of the people. . . . They are the only sure reliance for the preservation of our liberty. After all, it is my principle that the will of the majority should prevail." But what really stopped him was the fact that on the half-page left blank below the close of the letter, Thurston had written a note:

Jeff, when you do someday come to the point of wanting to read this book, I hope you'll be old enough to understand me. That's why I've buried this in the heart of the book, beneath a quotation that is the essence of my profession. If you've thought my motives toward you were founded on ill-will, I hope by now you can correct that impression. Only you can change your own mind.

I'd rather you believe me to be frankly selfish in wanting to instruct as many people as possible to the fullest extent of their capacities. You see, the will of the majority must govern me, too, and if the governing is poorly done, I will suffer along with you. Most particularly, as a teacher, I have committed myself to a special concern for anyone who shows keen imagination, as that is a commodity entrusted to us schoolmasters not to waste. If I let slide a pupil with such potential as yours, I have squandered some of the world's resources.

If you wonder what business this is of mine, then consider that none of us is so alone that his fate is not wrapped up with that of all the rest of us. How, then, can any of us dare neglect the rare energies with which we are armed to take part in this massive game? With this in mind, Jeff, believe me when I say I would have valued your friendship, but I had to value, even more, your wits.

Ben

For a long time, Jeff sat there as shivery as if he'd heard a voice from the grave—a voice speaking to him as one grown person to another. Nobody had ever made him feel this equal. It wasn't a pleasant feeling, because it had to take recognition of some shameful memories— childish bickering, pointless nastiness, hostility toward a man who . . . would have . . . valued his friendship.

Nobody had ever valued it before, not really. But Ben thought imagination was important, something not to be wasted. The Deacon just shucked it off as the work of a devil. Pa and the others—they'd never even understand a letter such as this, much less think of Jeff as a world's resource. Wits, too. Ben had believed in him all along. Jeff hoped the schoolmaster wasn't wrong.

Grimly he picked up the copybook and began to write the rest of the letter he had begun—not a graceful flow of words, all he could do was to put one plain sentence after the other. Starting a new paragraph, he went on:

> Nobody is going to be heard in this town as long as Pete Regan runs it. Ben Thurston was a good man, he tried to get them to talk up. Now he's disappeared. My pa is a good man, too, but he's been fired along with a lot of others. They were canned because they were going to talk to you about the timbering and all. Only now they won't. They're all scared.

Jeff started to write, *I'm not scared.* And then he knew it would be a lie, and Ben would have hated a lie in this letter. So he went on earnestly:

> I'm scared, too, because Ben Thurston's probably murdered and Sammy Yates is the law in town and he probably killed Ben and he certainly isn't going to arrest himself.

That sentence looked slightly too long. The whole letter was getting pretty long, and Jeff thought he'd better have another look for a suitable ending. Consulting the book again, he flipped through it at random—apparently

163

Ben had liked one letter best because the book fell open there just naturally. And right in the middle of a page Jeff saw a sentence so good he just had to use it:

> The tree of liberty must be refreshed from time to time with the blood of patriots and tyrants.

A few pages on, he found a thoroughly dignified ending.

> I am, dear sir, your obedient & Humble servant.

Then with just a slight inward tremor, Jeff signed his name.

14

*M*cNish had taken inventory of everything in the Danvers' house. The scrawny little redheaded man had come that first day and poked into the drawers and closets, setting down in his book each item that he considered of any worth.

He'd taken special note of Ma's mother-of-pearl dresser set that had been a wedding present. While the twins watched in open anguish, he had peered through the viewer of their precious stereoscope at the marvelous three-dimensional pictures of Niagara Falls, and had set the gadget down on his list for three dollars' worth— which showed that their uncle back in the East had really outdone himself to give them such an expensive Christmas present last year.

When McNish had eyed the handsome tortoise-shell combs in Becky's hair, she had faltered a protest.

"These were a gift. . . ."

McNish just shrugged and went on out to the kitchen to list each pot and pan, Ma's favorite skillet, Pa's rocking chair that they'd paid seven dollars for at the county seat—the storekeeper allowed them only two-fifty for it.

When he'd got through, he'd added it all up and stared at them through his little glasses that made his eyes look split in the middle.

"You're twelve dollars and fifty cents short," he announced in his scratchy old voice. "I'll take that in cash."

Pa swallowed visibly. With an effort, he said, "We hardly got enough to get us fare on the stagecoach into Idaho."

"I'm not interested in that," the storekeeper told him curtly. "You owe a debt, it's got to be paid. What else do you have to offer?" And again he looked at Becky's combs.

Without a word, she took them out of her hair and laid them on the table. There was dignity in the way she eyed him that even seemed to shame the hard-bitten little man.

"You can wear 'em until you leave," he told her ungraciously. "But come time to go, I'll be checking this list back, so don't try to sneak off with anything." He glanced toward Ma's jam closet. "You throw in that preserved goods and I'll even allow you some credit at

166

the store this week, so long as you don't eat too much."

Ma nodded numbly. They had completely forgotten that detail.

After he'd left, Pa had gone off without a word into the bedroom. These days he just lay there on the bed, looking up at the ceiling for hours. He was worse than Ma—she at least kept moving around the kitchen.

"It's going to be clean when I leave," she kept muttering. "I never would leave a place dirty." Not that Ma's kitchen ever had a speck of dust in it!

Once Jeff took Becky aside and asked her, "Wouldn't it be better if we went right now? What are we staying around for?"

"Don't say such a thing!" she pleaded miserably. "We've got to stay here as long as we can. Ben may be back—he's got to come back—" She bit her lip, unconsciously her hand went up to the combs, and Jeff realized whose gift they had been. It made him feel all the worse, because he was getting surer every day that Ben wasn't coming back, ever.

"I still think we should go," he insisted. "Pa's getting worse—it's like he's too sick to move."

Becky said defiantly, "He wouldn't be this way if he hadn't lost faith in Ben." She too was under strict orders never to mention the teacher in her father's presence again. These last days she'd been drifting around, doing the chores, pale and silent as a ghost girl. Now, she was full of resentment for a minute, but then it died out. "It's so hard on them—you can't blame them. They've got to get used to the idea. Don't hurry them."

167

All the same, Jeff was glad when the waiting was over and the day came. Worse to sit and think about the minute of leaving than to get up and do it.

They had precious few belongings in their small assortment of bundles as they marshaled themselves in the living room that last morning. Jeff had his own property tied up in a cardboard carton—the Jefferson book and a few other things. He had seen to it that the book was well hidden under a lot of junk when McNish made the rounds. Since then, he'd been considering how to trade it to the Scotchman for Becky's combs, but he had the discouraging feeling that McNish would end up with both if he tried that.

So now it was just a question of waiting until two o'clock, when the livery-stable man was to drive them and the other banished families over to the county seat in the big hay wagon. It was going to be as embarrassing as being hauled off to execution, Jeff thought, that slow trip along the Row, with everybody staring from behind their window curtains.

As they sat around the living room, Jeff was watching his parents anxiously. He thought Pa seemed to be taking hold a little.

"Where's the twins?" Danver asked once.

Becky, holding tight to the baby, who was whimpering, said, "They're in their room—they wanted to stay there until the last minute."

And Ma shook her head. "Poor kids don't know what this is all about."

"Won't learn any younger," Pa said curtly. "Maybe

they'll take a lesson from it, keep some quieter after this when they see what can happen if you open your mouth once too often."

But it was a good thing, Jeff protested wordlessly. *You said so yourself.* Aloud, he remarked, with an effort at cheerfulness, "Well, when we get to Idaho, we'll get into that Federation union, and . . ."

"That's enough talk about unions," snapped Pa. "Didn't you learn yet, either?"

Jabbed into silence, Jeff wandered over to the window. Glumly he said, "Here comes Mark Morse. Must be sent to check off the store list."

Pa cussed. For the first time in days, he let out a good one. And when the knock came, he opened the door with a fling that sent it back against the wall.

"Come on in and snoop," he said. "Bring your list. We didn't take nothing."

Jeff began to feel better. This was almost the tone of his father's voice as it had been before.

It was plain, though, that the Company man had more than the inventory on his mind. Glancing around him with a calculating curiosity, he walked into the room, bowed slightly to Ma and Becky, and then sat down, without being asked. Jeff thought he even seemed to be trying, secretly, to discover how much softness the sofa had—which wasn't much.

Then, as they stood, silent and hostile, grouped before him, even Morse seemed to grow slightly embarrassed. He stood up again and wandered over to the stove, made a pretense of being interested in the flue.

169

"That's in good condition," he murmured approvingly. "But does the stove give adequate heat for the house in the deep of winter?"

"Doesn't thaw the ice off the far windows, if that's what you mean," Pa told him curtly. "If you're thinking of moving in after we leave, I can just tell you the bedroom gets some chilly come twenty below."

Morse chewed his lip thoughtfully, moved over to the bedroom door. "May I?"

Pa flushed at the ironic courtesy of the man's manner. "Make yourself at home," he snapped. "It's no business of ours any more."

The Company man stepped into the bedroom, glanced at the old brass bedstead.

Pa followed with rising anger. "Ticking is some lumpy—if you don't dog-tire yourself with a good day's work, you notice it. Reckon you wouldn't sleep so good. Board's rotting out under that window, too. I got tin over it, but a driving rain still comes in. Reckon this house wouldn't be fancy enough for the likes of you."

Ma and Becky were glancing at each other fearfully. Afraid of—what? Jeff wondered. What more could the Company do to them?

Morse turned away from the bedroom, paused by the ladder.

"That leads to the attic," Pa told him fiercely. "Doubt if your young'uns would like it, though my boy has slept there all these years. Gets pretty cold when she goes below zero, and come summer, you could bake bread up there."

As Morse headed for the kitchen, the family followed closely.

With fine irony, Pa remarked, "I'm surprised to think you'd be interested staying in these parts, now that the trapping season's over."

Morse looked past him at Ma, made another of those cool little bows. "My compliments, madam, you keep a spotless house."

"Go ahead, look in the pantry," Danver shouted. "There's Ma's good preserves. I doubt your wife knows just how to jelly up a bucket of chokecherries, leastways not so good as Ma's."

But Morse went past the cupboards, heading for the door to the other bedroom.

"The twins are in there," Becky broke out, and went ahead of him to knock at the door.

"We'll be right out," a voice called sweetly.

Ma's face clouded with sudden suspicion. "That's a bein'-bad tone," she muttered, and went straight over to the door and opened it. What she saw made her gasp; she started to step back out again, but Morse was already behind her, looking over her shoulder. Politely but firmly he pushed the door wide.

The two girls stood there, all dressed from hat to shoes in their clean traveling clothes, scrubbed, pretty, and blazing with defiance. Around them, the walls of the room bore silent witness to their own personal feelings. In splendiferous crayon was created the most horrible gallery of ghoulish scribblings Jeff had ever seen—a round-headed, cross-eyed, red-and-green Pete Regan; a razor-backed, snaggle-toothed, purple McNish; Sammy Yates, all curly and slithery in choice yellow and orange; and finally a square-topped, owl-eyed, menacing figure in blues and blacks labeled respectfully "Mr. Morse."

In the horrified silence, Deb stuck her chin out, her eyes squinty with vengeance. "We just wanted to leave it real nice for whoever lives here after we're kicked out."

Dorrie went over to the dresser where the stereoscope lay. Carrying it straight over to Morse, she thrust it into his hands as forcefully as if she were stabbing with a deadly weapon.

"Here," she said, "I hope you like Niagara Falls."

With all the poise of princesses, they sailed through the kitchen into the living room, where they plumped down on the sofa, staring staunchly ahead as if daring fate to do its worst.

Hefting the viewer in his hand absently, Morse stared at the caricature of himself. As he turned back into the kitchen, he glanced around at them with an appraising look as icy as anything Jeff had ever seen. The four of them waited, and for that one moment they were really together.

As Morse seemed about to speak, a rap at the front door interrupted. Becky went to answer it, and a minute later the Deacon hustled into the kitchen to join them. He seemed surprised to see Morse, and the Company man looked outright irritated.

In answer to Danver's questioning look, though, the little preacher regained his composure and smiled. "I've news, good news, friend. I—ah, yes, let me sit down, thank you—I've been with Mr. Regan," he puffed. "All this morning. I've managed to talk him into giving you —all the men—another chance. Brother Danver, you've got a job again!"

Ma let out a little cry and sank weakly into a chair at the kitchen table. Pa blinked as if he couldn't quite take it in. Jeff was watching Morse—displeasure was written all over his face.

The Deacon was going on about how he'd naturally had to promise on behalf of the men that they would go back to work peaceably, never engage in disrupting activities again. "And I'm afraid, Brother Danver, that you'll not be drawing quite as good pay as before," he warned, "but on the other hand, if you all return in the proper spirit of meekness, Mr. Regan is almost willing to sign a pact with the miners. I've tried to explain to him that it's not an unreasonable wish for you to feel this need to belong to a group. He's beginning to listen to reason, although I must say he's a difficult man to argue with! However, I believe you'll have your—your union, as you call it, and your jobs, too, if you'll prove that you're in a willing mood to cooperate. You must convince him that there is no more violence in your hearts, that you won't go back to work in bitterness, even if—well, I should say you all may be assigned, for the time being, to—er—slightly less desirable work."

"What work?" Pa asked woodenly.

"Oh, mercy, I didn't ask that! One doesn't press one's luck!" the Deacon chided him.

"Of course not!" Ma burst out. "Deacon, it's been real, real good of you to do all this. We can't ever thank you!"

But when finally the Deacon had gone, Morse had gone, and the family was left alone to get used to the idea of going on living in the old familiar surroundings, Pa hardly seemed glad. As he sat at the table, leaning on his elbows, the violence that had seized him in the talk with Morse had burned out to ashes.

Jeff felt let down, too. "Does it mean everything will be just—like it was all along?" he wondered aloud.

"Shame on you, for even askin' such a question!" Ma cried. "We're lucky we ain't out travelin' off right this minute to the-Lord-knows-where!"

Becky looked worried, though. And Pa just sat there slouched down in his chair.

"I got to get to work!" Ma jumped up, her voice high and unnaturally bright. "I got to make us some lunch!" And then her look fell on the twins, standing aghast in the doorway.

"We aren't—going—to Idaho—?" Deb whispered.

"We *really* aren't?" Dorrie echoed.

"You two—!" Ma pointed a finger. "You step right in here and—and—" All at once she started to laugh, an

174

odd, rickety, helpless titter. Sinking down weakly opposite Pa at the table, she said, "You know, Harry, I ain't gonna spank 'em. This is one time—" She was laughing convulsively now. "Besides, they'll have their punishment—all those years ahead—lookin' at them awful pictures—" Putting her head down on her arms, she really let go. It almost sounded to Jeff as if she were crying.

15

*I*t was little short of miraculous how everything settled back into the old pace. By Saturday of that week, the wives, at least, were circulating with each other again as if it had all never happened—not even Pete Regan could keep women from gabbing. The kids played one-o'-cat in the street as noisily as ever. The men took their stint of work with no joy in it, but no complaint either. If they talked at all, it was a careful word about the weather.

There were a few reminders—the charred place where the cardhouse had stood, the unkempt grass growing higher every day in the yard of the schoolmaster's cabin. But nobody gave them a glance. It seemed to Jeff almost sinful the way they had sealed off all thought of the short time—that best, most hopeful time they'd ever known—into some dark place inside them to die.

The word on everybody's lips now was contentment —it was the Deacon's word. They were to content themselves, be grateful, give thanks, ask not, and be of good cheer. All of which made Jeff wonder, harder than he ever had before.

He reasoned that if his father really felt content, it would show in his eyes and bearing, the way his pride had, a few weeks ago. Now, speaking the words over and over didn't make it come true—there was no good cheer spreading through Pa, none at all.

Jeff wasn't sure just what sort of feeling had come upon his father, but sometimes he was reminded of a day long ago when he had watched two stablemen break a horse to harness. They had hitched the animal to a drag-board and let it plunge and kick until it was exhausted; then they'd buckled it into the shafts of a heavy wagon, put blinders on it, and laid on the whip. What little fight it had left was gone before they had run a mile, and it came back walking along, weary and docile. It had never kicked up again, either. Now, when he looked at his father, Jeff thought that Harry Danver had just about come into that last mile.

As the Deacon had predicted, the men of the erstwhile committee had been given the short end of the stick when they reported to work that first morning. One had been put with the boys on the picking tables, another had been assigned to sweep horse manure down in the entries, and a third to load it onto cars to be brought up-top. Two others were degraded to the back-breaking labor of loaders and put under the supervision of the lowly "furriners" from Scotch Coulee. But Regan had left the meanest job for Harry Danver—he'd been set to clean out the sumps.

It meant working alone down in the deep pits of the mine, crawling into half-caved-in entries where the foul-smelling water collected to be drawn off by the pumps. A thick muck of ooze and rock accumulated in these low places that had to be swamped out every so often—and the job hadn't been done for a long time.

That first night when he'd come home, Pa had hardly been able to touch his supper. Now, after four days of working in cold water ten hours at a stretch, he was starting to walk as if his feet hurt.

He didn't talk about it. But sometimes when Ma would be chattering along in all her newfound content-ment, Jeff would see his father look up at her with hopelessness spread over his face like gray paint. The boy wondered why the others couldn't see it. He kept thinking how Pa had warned them so plainly—*I'd just as soon pull the hole in after me.* It made Jeff want to help, somehow—to make up for the others' thoughtless-ness. With tentative, cautious sympathy, he tried to be around when his father was home, tried to talk to him.

This Saturday evening was the best chance they'd had. Ma and the girls were busy in the kitchen, all thrilled over the season's first wild currants, which Jeff had brought home from the hills that afternoon. He'd done a lot of figuring on that long walk, too. He hoped he could keep things as straight in his mind as they had been a few hours ago.

Looking across the front room at his father half sprawled out on the sofa, Jeff remarked, offhand, "It must be pretty awful down below these days."

Pa brushed the remark aside with a little weary flip of his hand. "What difference?"

"End of the month coming up, going to be short pay for everybody. Won't the others feel irked about it?"

"I didn't ask 'em," his father said sardonically. "Don't start me thinking about it, I don't want to think."

"Well, but it just seemed to me— I don't see why you all can't still do like Tom Winkler said, write a letter to the Federa—"

"Me write a letter?" Danver cut in with a mirthless laugh. "You trying to make fun of me, maybe—you and all that school learning?"

"Of course not!" Jeff protested warmly. "Listen, Pa, please don't be sore at me about that old business. It was like a—a—game, I guess. I know it was wrong to act dumb, but I'm not really so awfully smart, either—"

"I'll say you're not," Danver said heavily. "Talking about me writing a letter."

"Well, you could. Just a note to the Fed—"

"You stick that word back in your mouth and don't let it come out again," Danver ordered sharply. And even that much show of feeling did Jeff a little good.

179

There must still be a few embers banked down under that ashy surface.

Daringly, the boy went on. "If it worked out, over where Tom is—"

"We ain't over where Tom is," interrupted his father. "What you trying to do, fester things up again? Dog-gone if I don't think the Deacon was right, you got a devil in you."

"He said that to you!" Jeff asked in dismay. He hadn't taken the Deacon's threat seriously.

"Said a deal more. Said when a fool kid gets talking big, it's time his elders put a foot down. I reckon I been letting you get away with too much smartness lately."

Jeff knew he ought to take warning—Pa was certainly in no mood to get friendly tonight. And yet if he could only persuade his father that he really wasn't such a kid any more. . . .

"I didn't mean to sound smart," he apologized. "I just thought we could talk about some things."

"Like what?"

"Well, like this new contract, this union thing that Regan gave the men—"

"Don't pay no attention to it."

"But I'm going to have to sign it when I go back to work."

"You sure-as-shootin' are, and you do it and be still."

"But I don't see what good it can do. All it says is that you have to tell your grievances to Zack! Gosh-almighty, Pa, that's no better than before. He'll just get you canned if you let out a peep. And now you have to pay dues, too—"

"It's a dandy little union," his father told him acidly. "Like I said, you sign it and forget it."

"What I don't see is why everybody went along—"

"What difference does it make?" roared Danver. "Everything is the same as before, we got jobs, so who cares? Who cares? Forget all this wondering, forget it!"

Jeff started to protest, but the sound of steps coming up onto the porch made him check. He and his father both started up as they made out in the evening dusk that it was Sammy Yates who stood outside the screen door.

Danver walked over to confront him, made no offer to open up.

"Evening, Harry, I just dropped by to pay my compliments to your pretty daughter," Sammy said brashly. "Ain't you gonna ask me in?"

"You're not welcome here, Yates," Pa said. "She don't hanker to see you."

"Well, now, that's mighty unfriendly, especially since I just did you a favor, brought along some mail from the post office, it happenin' to be right on my way."

Danver looked suspicious. Jeff thought wildly of Ben. But neither of them was prepared for Sammy's next remark.

"This"—he took an envelope out of his pocket—"is a letter addressed to Jefferson—my, my!—Jefferson Danver, from Emerson Enterprises. That's the Company, in case you didn't know." And when Pa just stood staring, Sammy added with a grin, "Looks like we still got a little peanut-head tryin' to make trouble around this-here peaceful town."

Danver swung around. Under the terrible questioning of his eyes, Jeff had an impulse to shrink, and fought against it.

"What-for is the Company writing you?" his father asked tersely.

"I—I wrote them a little letter," Jeff replied feebly. "Back when you were fired—I just wanted to tell them they were wrong, to let a good man go—"

"Harry, that child's always busy takin' care of you!" Sammy marveled. "This time he could've took care of you real good if I hadn't happened to notice this letter before the bookkeeper got hold of it. That bookkeeper is an awful snoop, I tell you."

Inwardly Jeff was trying out several of his father's best cuss words. He had been careful enough to take his own letter over to the county seat to mail it; it hadn't ever entered his head he'd get an answer.

"Now," Sammy was going on briskly, "I reckon maybe you better ask me in and call Miss Becky, too, so we can see if she's really all that unfriendly."

Stiff with helpless rage, Pa unlatched the screen door.

"Don't let him in, Pa!" Jeff blurted out. "Tell him to chuck the job; we can still get out of here. Don't let him—"

"Shut your mouth," snapped Danver.

Sammy stepped in out of the dusk, sleek as a yellow

182

cat, stood there tapping the letter while Danver went to the kitchen door and summoned Becky. As the girl came in, she looked at Yates coldly, but she didn't say anything until Pa had told her the case in a few stark words.

"I don't see anything so wrong," she said with a tilt of her chin, "in a boy writing the Company to speak for his father. It's a free country, Sammy. What's more, stealing from the United States mails could land you right square in jail!"

"I doubt if Mr. Regan would look at it that way— such an unkind thought, and me just doing you all a favor." Idly he flipped the letter to Jeff. "So much for stealin'. Go ahead, Jeffie-boy, open it. Let's hear what the Company's got to say to you."

Before Jeff could decide what to do, Pa had ripped the envelope from his grasp and torn it open. In a hoarse monotone he read it aloud, one slow syllable after another.

"Dear Sir—
   Your favor of the twentieth received and we beg to inform that Mr. Emerson is at present out of the country. When he returns your letter will be referred to him.
                                    Yours truly,
                                       Secretary"

"Well, that's too bad," Sammy sighed. "All that writin' for nothin'. I heard you had a bright boy, Harry, but I never knew he was this bright. I do suppose Pete'll want to know about this. Maybe he'll make Jeffie his assistant in charge of letter writin'."

"What do you want, Sammy?" Becky asked with quiet contempt. "Come on out and say."

"Well, that's kind of rude." Yates leaned against the wall near the door, idly cracking peanuts and flipping them into his mouth. "Here I just come by to be friendly—ain't had much social life lately. Thought maybe you'd go to the dance with me tonight."

Jeff saw his sister go tense. It nearly twisted him off short inside, to be the cause of all this.

Then, steadily, Becky said, "All right. Give me a minute to fix up." And she went back into the rear part of the house.

They stood around stiffly until she came in again, dressed in her party dress. From the depths of his chagrin, Jeff threw her a miserable look. Becky nodded, just enough for him to know it was all right. As the two of them went out, the last thing Jeff saw was Sammy's hand squeezing her elbow with revolting familiarity.

Pa saw it, too, and turned a liverish color. As his glance fell on Jeff, the whole burden of his anger suddenly broke loose, his futility and outrage against everything. It piled down with the weight of forty tons of coal going down the chute.

"So . . . you . . . wrote a . . . letter," he muttered.

"I didn't think it would hurt." The boy shook his head regretfully. "You were already fired—"

"You didn't think. You did think. You can think. You can't. Who ever told you you had the *right* to think?" The words came faster and bitterer. "Git in the bedroom."

Backing away, Jeff fumbled for the knob of the door, his look fixed on what his father was doing. Danver was unbuckling his belt.

"Listen, Pa." He gathered together what dignity he could. "I reckon it was a mistake, but it was a well-meant one. I just was trying to say all the things Ben would have said to the Company—"

"I told you to shut up about Ben Thurston." Danver shoved Jeff ahead of him into the darkened bedroom.

"It's not wrong to try, Pa, is it?"

"Light the lamp."

Jeff did as he was told, but his hands were trembling. Turning again to face his father, he started once more, pleadingly. "I'm going to be a miner, too. I figured we *had* to try. I thought even if we had to go to Idaho —I still think it would be better in Idaho than staying here, being scared of Sammy Yates— Pa! You aren't going to—? Pa, I'm pretty old for that!"

"So you think," Danver said grimly. "And that's the whole blame trouble. Seems like my kid's been mixing in everything, catching spies, getting near killed, working folks up into a steam, and making folks get crazy ideas. Now, writing letters. Can't leave off stirring things up. All because you got the notion from a chicken-livered schoolteacher that you was some sort

185

of punkins! Well, you're nothing. You're a kid, a little smarty kid. And like the Good Book says, the sooner I smite the devil outa you, the quicker we can maybe have some peace. Drop 'em!' "

Without another word, Jeff wriggled slowly out of the shoulder straps of his overalls and let them fall around his ankles, bent over and took hold of his knees.

His father seemed to hesitate an instant, then brought the leather down hard. It nearly drove Jeff off balance, but he managed to stand still and clamped his teeth together as the strap fell again and again—a good dozen licks and then some, with Pa picking up speed as if the silence goaded him.

When he stepped back finally, Danver was breathing hard. "You can pull 'em up again," he said, "but the next time you get too big for 'em, they can be stripped down fast."

Left alone in the room, Jeff took his time getting back into the overalls. He felt as if he were burning —not just the welts on his backside, but the whole of him. His face felt hot as fever, but the hurt was not for himself.

When he did go into the front room, his father wasn't around. Climbing the ladder to the loft, Jeff went to his rack of clothes, took down a stout pair of corduroy pants and changed into them, moving tenderly. Putting on his heavy walking shoes, he decided on a good warm sheepskin jacket, for the nights were getting cooler all the time. Finally he stuck his hunting knife in his belt and his slingshot in his pocket.

For a minute, he hesitated over Ben's book—it had come to mean a lot. Not that he could get much of it yet—mainly he just liked to read that note over. But it was too heavy to carry a long way. And, as Jeff went down the ladder again and outside into the night, he didn't know how far he might be going.

16

*P*iano and fiddle music rollicked the dancehall, set feet pounding, hands pumping. Jeff stretched to look in the window a minute, one last time, at Becky. With cumbersome gusto, Sammy was see-sawing her around while she, light-footed and aloof, looked as if she weren't even aware of his big rough hand clamped on her waist. Jeff made himself watch a little while, even though the sight punished him a good deal worse than any licking.

When he finally did move on into the darkness, he was thinking of Becky—and of his father and mother. As he walked back up the Row past their house—he didn't think of it as his own any more—he felt that he was drawing nearer to understanding them than ever before. It was as if he'd been looking through the stereoscope with only one eye, so that everything had appeared flat and one-sided—and suddenly now he was seeing it all with both eyes open, discovering a depth that made big things stand out, near and important, and little things fade back into perspective. It was a new feeling, something he had to come to grips with before he could walk off along the tracks.

Instinctively he turned off up the path toward the schoolteacher's cabin—a place to hold up and think a minute, to tackle this thing he was on the verge of solving. Maybe, he thought wryly, there'd be a few leftover words still hanging in the air there, to help. He wished he could have remembered more clearly some of the things Ben had said. *The proof of a thing lies in the performance.* Slingshots . . . and people. As he came up to the darkened shack, he wondered sadly, for the thousandth time, what fate had befallen the teacher. Never having exchanged one kind word with Thurston, Jeff still couldn't understand why the sense of loss was so strong—

And then, as he stepped inside the cabin and closed the door, a wave of fright came over him—he knew he was not alone in the room. Not so much a sound as a sensation . . . of another presence. Stealthily Jeff fumbled in his pocket for a match, flicked it alight with a swift jerk of his thumbnail. And sank backward against the door as a hot torrent of relief poured over him, leaving him weak. For there on the cot lay Ben Thurston.

He was hard asleep—so plunged in exhausted slumber he scarcely seemed to breathe. Bearded, dirty, his clothes as rumpled as if he'd lived in them night and day the whole two weeks he'd been gone, Thurston hadn't bothered to undress except to take off his shoes. They lay on the floor beside the cot—what was left of them. Thin shoes, never meant for rough walking. Jeff looked at those battered feet and winced.

The match was scorching his fingers; Jeff blew it out and groped his way over to a chair. As he sat in the darkness, it took him a few minutes to get used to the idea that Ben was really back, that there was going to be a second chance at—everything. At spirit and dignity and self-respect, if the men would have it. Jeff thought of his father; and he had to doubt it. And yet, Ben didn't doubt it or he wouldn't have come back.

Why did he come back? As Jeff sat there, he felt like part of the pitch-dark. He felt faceless and nameless until he could come at answers and build them into some picture that he could be part of. For too long he hadn't fitted with anything, the mine or the school or his own family. And he thought, if there was a place to begin, it was with this one question: Why had Ben come back to Bearcat?

From some new point of detachment, Jeff considered his own throbbing body almost impersonally, tried to imagine how much worse injury Thurston had suffered,

190

and yet the more they piled on, the more determined the teacher seemed to stay. And it was borne in on Jeff that his own hurt was not the smart of his skin. There was the first answer.

Even as the teacher had lain aching on his cot, back early that summer, Ben had been steady inside. Because he had known why he'd been set upon, what sort of men had attacked him and who had sent them. He knew that he was a better man than they were, and that they were afraid of him.

But Jeff couldn't make his own case come that easy. He couldn't firm up inside with a good round feeling of defiance toward Pa. Harry Danver was a plain, honest man, always had been as kindly as he knew how to be. Again grief turned inside Jeff like a deep splinter —he kept remembering the unfocused look on his father's face, the ranting words and the fierce anger behind the blows. It was plain enough that Pa had been taking out a whole lifetime of disappointment on Jeff's rump, but why? He wondered if his father himself knew why.

And if you don't know the why of things, you're helpless, you come apart at the seams because there's nothing to hold you together. It was a frightening thought—to realize that he'd just watched a man start to crack in pieces. Better that they had gone on over to Idaho, anywhere. Even if they had come into hard times, there'd have been a certain amount of the good feeling left. Pa had certainly told off Mark Morse in fine style, even in their lowest moment. But then the

Deacon had come along with the job won back, and Ma had grabbed it up so quick—

There was another answer; they were coming swifter. For all she was a good woman, Ma didn't know the why of things—not even as much as Pa. So quick to borrow trouble, to haul back at every new idea. If she hadn't hung onto Pa and stopped him the night of the fire when he'd tried to rally the other men, Jeff thought they really might have stood their ground. Now she was acting blind-happy because her man had swapped his dignity for some more credit at the Company store. Not that Jeff could blame her—it was womanish to be fearful. Up to a man to hold firm and make his wife come along his way. Teach them. The way Ben had taught Becky. She'd been afraid of him once, but now she was proud—she could hold up her head, give up her fondest treasure. Because Becky had been prepared in the why of things.

Maybe, Jeff thought, his father should have explained more to Ma as he went along, but Harry Danver was never good at talk. And of course, you can't take the lead when you don't know about yourself. It was grinding disappointment—Jeff had thought for a while that Pa was almost as sure of himself as Ben, but then he'd never have let a woman get in his way. He'd never have yelled out that Jeff had no right to think—Pa had even admitted that he was running away from thinking.

And so am I, Jeff told himself harshly. Just running off, because I can't figure things. There was the toughest answer of all. You could keep running and running the rest of your life—it wouldn't ever give you the peace that the man sleeping over there on the cot must have. Somehow the fever inside Jeff was quieting down. It was even comforting to face the fact that he wasn't going to be able to figure things, not yet. With a good deal of scorn for himself, Jeff thought back to the night a few weeks earlier when he'd stood and loftily considered whether he should bother to go back to school. You don't ask yourself, shall I or shan't I be a peanut-head?

With growing excitement, Jeff thought ahead to some pretty good battles. He thought, Ben Thurston, if you and I come through all this, I'll come back and do your problems and toss a few back at you, too. I'll memorize the history dates, if that's what it takes, and I'll tell you about the generals of the Revolution and why they fought it. Maybe someday I'll even learn how to talk to Pa. . . .

And Jeff began to be able to think of himself as real again.

It was almost midnight when Jeff finally decided to rouse the schoolmaster. He hated to do it, but he was afraid of what might happen if the miners discovered Thurston's presence abruptly; he wasn't sure what they might do in the throes of their defeat, maybe without giving him a chance to tell his story. Pa hadn't allowed much pleading just a while ago.

Cautiously he lit the lamp and set it on the floor so that it wouldn't show bright from the windows—Saturday nights the town didn't go to bed so early as other evenings. Then he set about making a small fire in the stove, found some tea left in the cupboard and drew water for it. Finally, bringing a steaming cup over to the cot, he nudged Thurston gently.

When the teacher came awake, he started up with the instant wariness of an animal that's been sleeping on guard. When he saw Jeff, he sank back, a little dazed.

"I guess I got home . . . pushed so fast those last hours, I . . . lost track. . . ."

"I'm sorry I had to wake you," Jeff said, "but—"

"Is that tea?" Thurston struggled to sit up, took the cup gratefully and drained its hot contents as fast as he could down them. "Thanks. You manage to turn up whenever I . . . I've been . . ." Talking seemed to come to Ben with some difficulty.

"What happened to you?"

"Long story. There were more of them this time— my few precautions didn't do any good. They broke in here, disarmed me, and trussed me up like a sack of grain. Put me across a horse. . . . that was a long night, all night. . . ."

Jeff filled his cup again and the teacher finished it off.

"The worst of it was, they told me the union was going to get stamped out, said they knew all about the meeting at the cardhouse. They laughed—said wives and kids were most helpful with their gabbing, so I guess it just leaked out, little by little. Anyhow, they said the place was going to be burned down and the

194

blame laid on me." He broke off anxiously. "Did it—?"

"It happened. Just like that."

Thurston sighed wearily. "I had an idea they weren't bluffing, though I did hope the town wouldn't let them get away with it. Anyhow, somewhere down in Wyoming that next day, they took the blindfold off—did I mention that? Yes. They set me down afoot in the middle of a desolate land—fierce sun, straight-up. They told me to keep walking south if I wanted to reach water. Told me not to try to back-track, I'd die of thirst. And if I did make it up here, I'd be a wanted criminal."

"So you came back." Jeff smiled a little.

"I wasn't too worried by their threats, and I remembered hearing cattle a few miles back, thought it was only logical that they'd have some supply of water. It turned out to be true—I found some delectable mudholes. Food was more of a problem. I had to veer a good way off course to reach a homestead I saw in the distance. Got something to eat there, but they were poor people—they only had one horse to their name. So I went on afoot. After a couple of days I made it to a sheepherder's camp. He gave me some more food and—I just kept walking." He stuck out a swollen foot and chuckled.

Jeff hated to put an overcast on the schoolmaster's determination. "I'm afraid you're going to have to walk a little way more, Ben. It would be dangerous for you to stay here."

195

Thurston shook his head. "Bring Regan on! Let him pull his false charges against me. I'd like to get that big ox into a courtroom."

"It's not just him," Jeff said reluctantly. "It's the men. They—they turned against you pretty hard."

The teacher looked up sharply in disbelief. "They wouldn't fall for Regan's rigged-up plot."

"It was rigged pretty well." Jeff went on unhappily to tell him of the events of that night. When he came to the finding of the scrap of paper, he felt in his pocket. He'd brought it along with a whole handful of odds and ends he'd transferred from his overalls.

Thurston puzzled over it a minute, then looked up frowning. "Why, this is from a letter I wrote to the State, weeks ago, asking for funds to be granted to open a public school here—a school that would be independent of the mine ownership. Somebody has torn off the first two letters of this word—it originally read 'unhappily,' and the rest of the final sentence would have ruined their case. I wrote, '. . . can be led to their own downfall *unless more teachers are brought in to give them the tools of self-decision—*' or something like that. This"—he shook the piece of paper— "must have been stolen from the government mails."

"That can happen," Jeff agreed dryly. He went on to tell of all that had followed since the night of the fire, leaving out the story of the letter—he hoped he wouldn't have to tell about tonight's encounter with his father.

Thurston listened with growing concern, then anger

196

and—discouragement. He couldn't hide it. When Jeff was through, he shrugged. "I was afraid the heart might go out of the men, if they were ever convinced that I'd betrayed them. I knew they might be confused— that's why I pushed on so hard to get back as soon as possible."

"It would be better if they were confused," Jeff said. "They've already settled for the old way, Ben, and they're full of hard feelings. You've got to keep clear of them until we can work out some way to make them listen again. I've been thinking, maybe you could write the Federation and then, with them on our side, you could come back into town. . . ."

Thurston was shaking his head. "It's no good, Jeff. If the men haven't the gumption to stand up to the Company, they won't be able to assert themselves with a big rough outfit like the Federation. They'd be taken over, told what to demand and what sabotage to engage in. Eventually they'd be worse slaves than they are now— ahead in money, maybe, but no more able to stand on their own feet. No, Jeff, I'm going to stay right here and convince them I didn't desert the cause."

"And you'll get lynched," Jeff retorted.

"Look, worthy adversary, get yourself home and kindly tell your father I'd like to see him. Tell him—"

"I can't tell him anything! I tried to talk to him just tonight, and you know what he did? He took his belt to me! Besides, I'm not your adversary, either. I read what you wrote in that book. But if you aren't going to believe me—" All at once Jeff's voice went dry on

197

him. Of all people, he couldn't bear to have Thurston make light of him.

The schoolmaster eyed him hard for a minute, and then the dark-bearded face took on a curious look that was part smile, part wonder. "You found what I wrote. . . ." he murmured.

"You said you valued my wits," Jeff reminded him soberly.

With a small gesture of acknowledgment, Ben held out his hand.

Jeff gripped it.

"All right," Thurston said, "since I can't stay here, what do you want to do with me?"

The town was only a string of shadows as Jeff and Ben moved away from it, up a path so dim the boy had to feel his way by memory. As they passed behind Pete Regan's mansion, they saw lamplight deep inside it; Jeff breathed better when they were past and up on the high crest of the bench. Leading the way down the other side, he cut across the old flat place where they used to play shinny, went on down past a couple of old mine buildings fallen into disrepair. Underfoot, he felt the patch of concrete where the showerhouse had once stood, and at last brought Thurston to stand in front of the black hole that slanted away deep into the earth, the gaping mouth of the Old Mine.

"It's sealed about forty feet below here," Jeff told him in a hushed voice, "so there's no chance of gas getting you. And hardly anybody ever comes here except kids. They don't go into the shaft much." In fact, he'd never been, himself, before. Now he lit a match and walked in boldly, the teacher limping after him.

"Why did they close it down?" Ben asked.

"Because an explosion tore up everything below," Jeff explained. "Killed thirty-seven men on the second level, six down on third. They're still down there, too —couldn't get them out. That's why kids don't fool around in here—it makes you feel funny." Briskly he took the blankets they had brought and spread them on the floor of the shaft. "It's a slopey bed, but it's safer than down in town tonight. I'll come up tomorrow morning with food—I'll see if I can find Pa's old razor."

Thurston laid a hand on his shoulder, looking down in the light that was spreading from the late moonrise in the east.

"It's pretty late for you to be out," he said. "Take care going home."

"Don't worry." Jeff pulled out the slingshot and tapped it in his palm. "I'm armed."

He kept it in his hand on the way back, a couple of good stones in the other. One move from the shadows, and he'd put a good nick in somebody. He was particularly on guard as he went along again behind Regan's house. Below it, he cut across behind the store and rounded a corner almost into the arms of someone hurrying in the opposite direction. In the moonlight, Jeff recognized the Deacon.

"Gracious, lad! What possesses you to be out so late?"

"I—I've just been with a friend," Jeff said evasively. After his father's quoting the Good Book on the treatment of devils, Jeff wouldn't have given the Deacon two nickels for a dime.

The little man caught him off guard, though. Knowingly, he said, "I'd imagine you've been with Ben Thurston."

It took Jeff a minute to organize his surprise, and as he stammered for an answer, the Deacon chuckled.

"Yes, indeed, I suspected he was back. I was tremendously relieved when someone told me there was a light in his cabin. I hurried right over to see him as soon as possible, but he'd gone again. Stove was still warm, tea in the pot, so I assumed that someone had warned him that the temper of the men is a bit uneasy. Good thing, good thing. I hope he has retreated to a safe spot. I must see him before he ventures into town."

Jeff was thinking it was just as well he'd got Ben out of there when he did—for some reason, he wasn't sure the Deacon would handle things right with the men. Of course, the question of how he himself was going to get them to listen to him was one that Jeff hadn't solved yet.

"If you'll just tell me where he is," the Deacon was going on, "I'll go to him right away. No energy must be stinted to help set matters right."

"Why would you want to see him?" Jeff asked uneasily, trying to edge away; whether by chance or

the Deacon hit him. Now his jaw ached, but his head was clear. Too clear. He could even ‚detest himself for having pulled the prize mistake of all time—thinking the Deacon was a meek, silly little man.

He was going on talking now in brisk, chilling tones. "Don't be too proud of yourself, Sammy. If you'd seen that light and come to me a few minutes earlier, we'd have caught our bird. Now we've got to pry it out of our young guest and take time to go hunting—time which we don't have to lose right now."

"I still don't like it," Regan grumbled. "Now the kid's going to know so much about you and this whole business, we can't let him go."

"Suppose you leave Jeff to me," the Deacon said smoothly. "That's what you're paying me for."

"I'm paying you for good advice," snapped Regan. "I don't see why you told me to take the brat's father back in the mine. If we'd kicked the lot of 'em out, we wouldn't have to worry about the teacher now, one way or the other."

"Wrong again, Pete. There's no better way to discourage men than to show them the ignominious sight of their erstwhile elected representatives crawling on their bellies. The only real leader they ever had was the schoolmaster, and, if you remember, I did counsel you to remove him more permanently. I was afraid he'd be back to plague us—crusaders never give up."

"I tell you, I don't want any outright killing. You could get my neck stretched for a thing like that," Regan said flatly. "Makes me feel itchy—"

"Sure, Pete." The Deacon laughed. "I know. And when we're done with the boy, he'll be taken care of in such a way that you won't be involved, and he won't be back. Oh yes, we'll do it gently, Pete."

"I'd like the job myself," Yates said. "Me, I'm not scared of no neck-stretchin'. Who's gonna miss a dumb kid?"

"Sammy, don't underestimate our little package here." The Deacon sounded irritated. "Jeff has the aggravatingly healthy reasoning powers—not to say daring —of a black-haired son of a hardheaded Welshman. He's put me through some uneasy times, first when I thought he might have recognized me along with you at Pete's house that night, and then when he saw through one of my best-laid schemes. He even had the obnoxious curiosity to go clear through that trash barrel. Heaven knows what else he found there—he claims it's proof of Thurston's innocence. Now he's managed to get to the teacher ahead of us and warn him out of town. So I say it was fortunate and necessary that we take him in hand tonight and find out what he knows."

"What makes you think he'll tell where Thurston is?" asked Regan uneasily.

"Oh, come, Pete! He's just a youngster. It won't be hard to persuade him. Sammy, see if our young man isn't thoroughly wide-awake by now. From the clench of his fists, I'd say he's been listening to us."

With as much composure as he could muster, Jeff

204

sat up, blinking a little in the lantern glare. He saw that he was in the cellar of the dancehall—it was full of old leftover decorations from long-ago dances, and they had hung some of the discarded draperies over the windows. It was close and quiet in the basement room; outside—even quieter.

Sammy stepped forward and hauled the boy to his feet, held him helpless with his arms pinned behind him.

Staring up into Regan's florid face, Jeff met those coppery eyes and wouldn't let himself look away.

"Where's the teacher?" Regan asked, his lips hardly moving.

Jeff didn't answer.

Sammy shook him as easily as shaking a sack of sugar. "Speak up when you're spoke to."

The Deacon said kindly, "Yes, lad, tell us and save yourself some discomfort. Sammy, show him—just slightly."

With a grip like a vise, Yates clamped one of Jeff's arms up behind the small of his back, forcing it higher. . . . The shooting pain brought a qualm of nausea over Jeff; he buckled up in Sammy's hold, but kept his mouth clamped shut. It was his only chance of staying alive, even for a short while. At least, he had his own ideas about the Deacon's "gentle" plans for him.

"I tell you, this is going to take time," snapped Regan, "and we've got none to waste right now. We got not a minute to spare until those ledgers get doctored up to balance right."

"True." The Deacon motioned Sammy to let up. Jeff's knees would have folded if the Deacon hadn't shoved forward a chair.

"Takes time to change figures and make 'em tally," Regan was going on, worried. "Why in the name of mud the Company had to send the auditors down now, when they weren't due for a month—" He let out an ugly word.

The Deacon nodded. "Yes. Why? That bothers me, too."

"And they want 'em fast, too. They tried to get me to show 'em today—maybe you think I didn't have my hands full, stalling. Told 'em the bookkeeper didn't have his posting up to date. But come morning, Sunday or no, they're going to be at the office at ten o'clock, waiting."

"And the books will be ready, Pete."

"But I'm worried you can't do a slick enough job that quick."

The little man nodded. "I can. You go to the office and get them, take them to your house, and I'll be there by the time you are."

"And leave the kid here?"

"I can't think of a better place. Sammy will keep him company."

Regan turned to go up the stairs, but glanced back. "Remember what I said. I don't want any trouble over this kid. They may be missing him by now."

"Don't worry," the Deacon insisted impatiently. "It's

easy enough with a small ration of brotherly love to convince these fools of practically anything. I'll simply implant it in their minds that he has run away. I'm more worried about the teacher—to be on the safe side, you'd better stop by Morse's rooms on your way and tell him to keep an eye out to intercept Thurston in case he should take it into his head to come in town."

Regan nodded. "About time that Pinkerton started to earn his pay." He stamped on out, leaving the Deacon to turn his attention back to Jeff.

As he looked down at the boy, there was no slightest flicker of mercy in those eyes—instead of their usual velvety softness they were shining hard, like coals.

"Well, laddie," he said, "you've pried and poked yourself into the middle of a business that's rolling far too high and wide to be stopped by the tampering of a snub-nosed boy—or a long-nosed scholar. So you will tell us where Ben Thurston is and the two of you will be eliminated from the pleasant scene of Bearcat—to such a distance that you won't be back. If you choose to cooperate, it's even possible you may be allowed to make your departure alive. Care to speak up? Quickly, now!"

Jeff set his teeth and sat silent.

"Then it will have to be the hard way, my boy." To Sammy he said, "Tie him to the chair—there's clothesline over there. Under no circumstances take it upon yourself to question him until I come back. Your methods are decidedly heavyhanded. I don't want him too badly injured to tell us what we need to know."

As Sammy set about binding his hands to the sides of the chair, Jeff considered lunging and struggling, trying to make some sort of fight, but he knew it would be hopeless and would probably result in his getting hit again just when he needed to keep all his wits clear. So he sat still and hoped they would forget that at the first sound of footsteps outside, he could let out one terrible yell. They didn't forget. Once his hands were secured, the Deacon got out a handkerchief, forced it into his mouth as easily as bridling a horse, and tied another over it for good measure.

"Remember, Sammy, he can still make some noise. Stay with him and keep him quiet."

Yates nodded sullenly. "Sure, if there's any dirty work, I get to do it."

Jeff actually dreaded to see the Deacon mount the stairs and step out into the night. While they'd been talking, he had secretly tested the ropes on his wrists; they were absolutely unyielding. It was a bad feeling —to be unable to move his hands, to have to sit here, stuffed and stuck and helpless.

Moodily, Sammy dug into his pocket for a handful of peanuts; leaning against the wall, he studied Jeff as he cracked open the shells and tossed the nuts into his mouth.

"You," he grunted. "You been a real meddler all right, snoopin' around Regan's, gettin' me in all that trouble. I'd have still been havin' a nice easy life if it wasn't for you. I'd be havin' fun—I ain't had any fun for a long time. Folks don't speak to you, act like you're dirt. Take a girl to a dance—I'd as soon've danced with a clothes dummy. Wisht your hoity-toity sis could see you now; that'd bring her down off her high horse. Slapped me, she did. All I wanted was a little good-night kiss and she slapped me, right on the face. I don't take kindly to that. Here—" He stepped forward abruptly and swung his open hand in a blow that jarred Jeff's skull. "You can give her that back for me when you see her—except, I forgot, you ain't gonna see her."

Prowling the room and chomping peanuts furiously, Sammy seemed to be working up steam. The basement, which served to house the big coal furnace that heated the dancehall, had evidently been a catch-all for years. It was full of odds and ends of furniture, cooking utensils, laundry tubs—in one corner was a pile of books. Jeff was almost sure they were Ben's. Restlessly Sammy circled the place, then came back to stand looming over the boy. Jeff steeled himself.

The yellow-haired man snickered. "Scared, huh? Oh, I ain't gonna hurt you—yet. In fact, the Deacon's got me wrong—I wouldn't injoor a hair of your head. There's plenty of neat little ways to make a body feel talkative. I could show you a few, except I can see you ain't real conversational right now. Fact, you don't hardly look comfortable. Maybe your shirt's buttoned a mite too tight." He loosened Jeff's shirt at the throat, leaned over judiciously and stuffed a handful of cracked peanut shells down the back of the boy's collar. "That's better."

Wandering on around the room again, Sammy unearthed a dilapidated old sofa, hauled it out of the tangle of junk and sat down on it, scratching himself.

"Must be irritatin' not to be able to scratch when you feel like it," he observed. "Take them peanut shells, now. That's what I mean when I say it's the little things that add up to makin' a body want to talk and talk. Oh, not yet, Jeffie-boy, not till the Deacon gets here. But when he does come, well, let's see what we'll do first. You don't mind if I tell you my ideas? I swear, I ain't talked to anybody for so long." He leaned back, yawning.

Jeff's back was wet with sweat; the shells prickled and itched all right, but not half so acutely as Sammy's careless words. He was untying his boots now—picked a cocklebur off his socks and regarded it with interest.

"There's a useful little thing," he remarked. "Must've picked it up in the lot out back—there's a million of 'em out there. Let's see now, I'd say about the touchiest part of your fizz-eek is maybe the bottom of your feet, right there in the soft part of the arch, wouldn't you? It'd be right fun to spread out a good layer of these on the floor—ouch! Them prickers is sharp as a needle! Yes sir, put 'em all over the floor and let you play a little barefoot hopscotch. Blindfold, natcherly. No, I got a better idea than a blindfold. You ever get soap in your eyes, Jeffie-boy? Hurts fierce. Can't see a thing. They got plenty laundry soap upstairs in the store...."

Oh, Sammy was a very humorous fellow.

Was it ten hours—or ten days—later? Jeff wondered. In the curtained-off depths of the basement, time seemed fixed and clammy. Yates had finally drowsed off to sleep, leaving Jeff to some gruesome speculations. The straight chair was a torment in itself; if he slumped, his back began to ache. And he was too tired to sit erect. He kept nodding and yet he had to keep awake. His one chance, the only chance he'd been able to figure, was to listen carefully for the first sound of near foot-steps outside and then try to groan good and loud. Sammy would wake up, of course, and stop him, but maybe someone would have heard and be curious enough to come searching.

The most disheartening thought of all was that they probably wouldn't even be looking for him. Finding his heavy clothes gone, they would assume he'd left home for good, just as he'd meant to, and they would never even know that he'd met with foul play. Unless Thurston somehow got past the Deacon's clever pitfalls and sneaky words long enough to speak to the towns-people, but Jeff hadn't much hope for that. Grim as the thought was, he wasn't even sure that when the time came he'd be able to stand Sammy's little tricks without giving up his secret.

He looked across at the snoring deputy, who

sprawled loosely on the sofa. Sammy was beginning to get fat in the belly.

Vaguely Jeff wondered how a person could ever think so much of the easy-come money that he'd be willing to cut himself off from every decent man and woman in town. He thought Sammy had seemed a little puzzled about it himself. Was it possible, Jeff wondered, that Sammy had been sucked down into a mess like this without knowing it? Like wading in a sump where poison kept trickling in, poison from Regan, from the Deacon, until Sammy found himself mired and poisonous, too? He thought, a little ruefully, of how he'd once almost wished he could be like the sagging, sour-faced man asleep on the divan.

Outside, steps grated on the ground as someone passed—a good way off, too far away to spend that one short chance on. But Jeff thought it must be morning. He'd chewed the gag down into as small a lump as possible and shifted it as far to one side as he could. Now he got ready to make what sound he was capable of as soon as someone came close. Unfortunately, the cellar was under the rear half of the dancehall, away from the street, though ducts from the furnace led forward beneath the floor to all parts of the upstairs room.

It seemed as though no one would ever chance by. And then, finally, Jeff did hear steps coming closer. He held his breath, ready to burst forth with as much noise as possible, when he realized that the steps were coming straight here, and a minute later the door was opened —by the Deacon. Jeff went limp with ultimate defeat.

Sammy roused up as the little man came down the steps.

"Asleep, Sammy? That was very heedless of you!"

"Well, I'm tired," grumbled Yates muddily. "Man's got a right to catch a nap. I'm glad you come—let's grind the stuff out of the kid and get this over with."

"Nonsense, it's almost ten o'clock—the streets are full of people. They're already collecting out in front for the prayer meeting. I've got to go up right now. I had hoped to get back sooner, but Mr. Regan's accounting was somewhat more involved than I had anticipated. However, it's in good shape, I think. As soon as I dispose of the sheep-eyed flock upstairs, we'll go to work on our subject here, then proceed to finish with Mr. Ben Thurston once and for all. Meanwhile, need I explain that you must stand by to stop any slight sound he may make while there are people up above? Is that so difficult to comprehend?"

He spoke in a biting tone that made Sammy flush.

"Also," added the Deacon, "while I don't expect any trouble, all the same, should anything happen that this game blows up on us, if you hear matters getting out of hand, be prepared to settle the boy, permanently, rapidly, and quietly. We want no talkative young witness around to complete a case against us, Mr. Regan's squeamishness to the contrary. You understand, Sammy, this is only in case of emergency."

"Such as what?"

"I don't know. I'm still puzzled over this business of the auditors showing up, just when we were getting things back in hand. Of course, the books are in perfect order now—" He shook his head, frowning, and went back up the stairs hastily.

As soon as they were alone again, Sammy turned on Jeff irritably. "Every time I get around you, I get in Dutch!" He tweaked the boy's nose cruelly. "Go on, holler. I wisht you'd try!"

But Jeff sat hopeless, as, from above, came the inward trooping of feet—the people of Bearcat gathering to listen to their dear counselor, all unaware of the tight little twosome down in the cellar.

They heard the Deacon take his place, just over-head, and through the open furnace ducts came the familiar gentle tones, carrying plainly into the quiet of the basement.

"Dear friends, let us first sing a hymn. . . ."

18

"*G*ood people, I'll just write today's text here on the blackboard. . . ."

Jeff knew exactly what was going on upstairs; this was the way the Deacon always started his prayer meetings, putting up the "text" in chalk so that they wouldn't forget it.

Now, he was going on sermonizing. "I'm taking this right from the Good Book: 'What is man? He is no more than the sheep and oxen, yea, the beasts of the field.' Oh, you poor sinners, consider that and be not proud!"

"Begging your pardon, Deacon, I got to ask you something."

From the midst of his paralysis of despair, Jeff recognized that voice, even though it sounded a long way off upstairs, somewhere at the other end of the hall. Still, there was no mistaking—it was his father's.

"Brother Danver, let your private troubles wait until after meeting," the Deacon reproached him. "This is no place to ask questions."

"I say it is," Danver insisted. Jeff could hear the little shocked murmur from the people up there. Miserable as his own situation was, he could still wonder dimly at his father's daring to talk up like that.

"I say," Pa was going on, "that you told me a wrong thing not two days ago, and I want to ask you where-at in the Bible it says it's right to lick the devil out of somebody, and anyhow, how can you tell for sure they got this devil in 'em? I need to know, Deacon!" Pa sounded strained with torment. "I want to see it myself. Because it seems to me when a body does a right thing, like the Bible preaches, he ought to feel good inside. And I don't feel good inside."

"Dear friend, calm yourself," said the Deacon smoothly. "Your reward will come in heaven for whatever good you've done. Now you know you can't expect to collect it on earth, don't you?"

"I can't out-talk you, Deacon, but I know something's wrong." Jeff heard his father's voice rise. "I may be just a dumb miner, but since I been listening to you, I been getting downhearted. Yes sir, I'm gonna speak this out! I acted mean to my boy yesterday, and now he's gone—run off. Likely I'll never see him again. He didn't do nothing except show some spunk, and I whipped him for it. Why should I whip the spunk out of my boy? Do I want him to turn out like me, eating coal dust and crawling to the likes of Regan?"

That put them in a flurry upstairs.

Sammy snickered. "Your pap's gettin' pretty big for his breeches, gonna wisht he hadn't. Deek don't like folks talkin' up like that."

"You asked it yourself, Deacon! You got it writ right there—'What is man?'" Danver was rushing on hotly. "It's what we was, up to the night of that fire, and what we ain't been since. And me, I'm through with not being. I wouldn't walk back into that mine to Pete Regan's tune if I starved and my whole family with me. There's worse things than starving."

"Sister Danver," called the Deacon loudly, "you hear your husband, threatening you and your poor little ones with an awful fate. You'd better take this poor man home. I think he's coming down with the devil himself."

"Ma's through butting in—we had that out last night," Jeff heard his father say flatly. "She's with me, and nobody is gonna take us home. It's no devil, either, Deacon—seems to me you been dealing out these devils pretty free lately. I dunno why. But I do know I should've stood up before this. Because when you tell me I'm low as a beast, I want to say, 'No, I'm not.' Well . . . what are the rest of you sitting there so bug-eyed for? You want to feel rotten inside? Do you like it? Maybe it takes having your kid run off from home. A good kid, too. Any time you start lickin' a good kid, you ain't a whole man no more."

Jeff was swallowing hard, his throat so full of pride that it was nearly choking him. And even though he knew it wasn't ever going to be, he wished he could see Pa just once more for a minute or two.

"If you've done something to send your son from you," the Deacon roared wrathfully, "blame not the wise words of the Good Book or you'll sizzle in eternal fire, brother."

"I ain't blaming nobody but myself," Danver said, firm and loud. "I blame myself a-plenty for listening to your speechifying. I don't think you're much of a deacon. I don't hardly think you're a deacon at all. You never would say where you come from. Anybody can call hisself a deacon—or anything. So I'm askin': What-all church did you ever see the inside of?"

"Blasphemer!"

And then the Deacon's high, angry voice was drowned out by a deeper one. "There's no blasphemy in that question. Are you afraid to answer it, Deacon?" The challenge came from somewhere off at the far end of the room. Jeff thought it sounded like—and then he knew. It was Ben Thurston!

For an instant there was dead silence upstairs, as if they sat stunned, probably not even recognizing the ragged, bearded man as their schoolmaster; then all sorts of pandemonium started to break loose. There was shuffling of feet, babbling of voices, hard to tell what their reaction was. Jeff looked at Yates.

The smile was gone from Sammy's face; he was listening closely, glancing at Jeff with the grimness of an executioner. "So the teacher came back all by hisself," he muttered. "We won't be needin' you, after all."

"Thurston," the Deacon thundered wrathfully, "I should think you'd be ashamed to show your traitor's face in this community that you've deceived so disgracefully."

"If I had turned traitor I wouldn't have come back, and you know it, Deacon!" snapped Ben. "You're not that dumb—in fact, I'm starting to wonder just how smart you may have been through all this, with your poor-mouth talk. What Harry just said made sense to me. But there's no time to argue that—a boy is missing and he has not run away, I'd stake my life on it!"

"He's stakin' yours, too," Sammy commented. "Ain't that nice of him?" He had picked up a piece of the clothesline and was fiddling with it; Jeff saw a noose taking shape in his hands. So that was the way it would be. . . . He tried not to watch, tried to focus on what Thurston was saying.

"Jeff came to me in my cabin last night shortly after I got to town. He told me the people had turned against me. I hardly believed him, but when I heard all that had happened here the night I was abducted, and learned that you hadn't stood up and fought for your union, I realized that the old evil forces were still very much afoot. Since I didn't want to be seized again and transported a hundred miles away before I got to speak to you, I let Jeff show me to a hiding place for the night.

He left me about midnight and promised to come back with food this morning. When he didn't show up, I came on down to town, and . . ."

"This is fabrication of the thinnest paper!" the Deacon interrupted scornfully. "What fools he must think we are, to believe that he was kidnaped and then let go again, seized one moment and freed the next. Came back to his cabin—left his cabin. A flimsier story I've never heard!"

"There's nothing flimsy about this—" Thurston evidently showed them something, for there was a commotion of exclamations. Then Jeff heard his father speak in a stricken, frightened voice.

"That's his, all right. Where'd you get that, Ben?"

"Now we must have slingshots!" cried the Deacon with fine sarcasm. "What a way to ridicule a holy Sabbath meeting—"

"This is Jeff Danver's slingshot," Thurston cut in hard, "and the Sabbath is a fitting time to go to the boy's rescue if he's in danger. I found this out in back of these buildings, not twenty yards from your house. Maybe you have some good reason for trying to override me, Deacon, just as you tried to shout down Harry Danver when he called you on your preaching. He was dead right, too. If the rest of the people in this room had two grains of his courage, they'd admit that everything he said is so."

"Now wait up, teacher," somebody protested. "That ain't fair. We was doing all right on courage until you kited out—I mean we thought you did—"

As a little bicker of voices sprang up in the meeting hall, Sammy was scanning the beams of the cellar. Where one had warped, there was a crack between the top of it and the floor of the dancehall. Bringing over a stool, he got up on it and threaded the rope through the opening.

"—and I will prove exactly what happened," Thurston was calling out in a clear, penetrating voice that stilled the crowd little by little, "including a certain piece of trickery involving a letter of mine which was cleverly torn to fool you into thinking I had plotted against you. But this will all have to wait. The point is that Jeff Danver may be in danger this minute. Are you going to sit idle while the boy is spirited off, or hurt?"

"If I have to tear down every house in town," Pa said wildly, "I'm gonna find him. And I'm gonna start with the Deacon's place."

"Brother Danver," screeched the Deacon, "you seem full-bent on ending up in jail, and all your lawless friends with you."

That seemed to scare them a little; they muddled around. Jeff thought sickly that they'd likely be too late anyhow; Sammy had got the rope over the beam now. In a passionate burst of agony and determination, Jeff gathered his feet under him and, with all the force he could muster, propelled himself—chair and all—headlong into Sammy on the stool. They went down together in a muffled crash.

As the deputy floundered on the floor, Jeff let out the

loudest groans he could manage, straining to make himself heard, but his efforts went unnoticed in the seething of the people above.

Sammy shook free of the rope and scrambled up. "You little buzzard," he swore, "I'll finish you off with my own hands. . . ." And then he stopped short, for someone had come down into the cellar, lightly and quietly. Mark Morse stood taking in the situation with those cold eyes.

"Stop that," he ordered. "This business upstairs is more important. I'll take care of the boy. You go and get Regan, tell him things are getting out of hand. Tell him to come down here, and hurry."

"I don't take orders from nobody but Pete." The deputy scowled uncertainly.

"And Pete," said Mark Morse, "takes his orders from me. Now do as I say and do it quickly."

Wide-eyed, Sammy seemed about to ask questions, but something in the man's look stopped him and he went off, scowling and puzzled.

When he had gone, Morse picked Jeff off the floor, but something was happening above that made him go over to the nearest duct opening and listen closely.

"Can they put us in jail, Ben, if we go search Regan's house?" a voice asked timorously.

"If the boy is missing," the Deacon exhorted them furiously, "this is a matter for the law."

"We can't go to the law, we got no law," yelled somebody.

"Tell us what to do, Ben."

The teacher answered angrily. "Do what Harry just said a few minutes ago—look at yourselves and do what'll make you feel like a man!"

"That's sinful talk!" the Deacon screamed. "The Good Book says the Devil will come to tempt you, but you must stone him out of the temple."

"This is no temple," Thurston came back—he was more worked up than Jeff had ever heard him. "And a man is no preacher just because he puts on a black suit and pretends to offer prayers. To corrupt the most sacred calling that a man can have, to use the trust of simple people to lead them into unhappiness, is vicious profanity. Even I refused to think you were anything worse than a bumbling pessimist until I came here today and saw that text of yours written there. Where do you get your texts, Deacon? What is this Good Book you quote from? Not the Bible, that's certain."

"Silence! Blasphemer!"

"Care to give us chapter and verse on that miserable concoction you've put there on the board?"

The men were firming up. ". . . Yeah, I don't feel like no beast of the field. . . ."

". . . tryin' to call me a ox . . ."

"Oh, unfaithful"—the Deacon sounded desperate—"you will suffer a terrible penance someday!"

Thurston had evidently walked forward, for his voice came from close above now, as he said, with ringing clarity, "I'll tell you what the Bible says on the subject—if anybody out there has one, he can check me—because the Eighth Psalm is one of my long-time inspirations.

In the fourth verse, the question is asked: 'What is Man?' And the next verse comes back, strong and beautiful: 'Thou hast made him a little lower than the angels and hast crowned him with glory and honor.'"

"It says so!" cried a woman's voice. "I found it! Right here!"

"Then I reckon from here on it's up to us!" a man shouted.

Morse was moving over to Jeff's side, opening his pocketknife as he came. The boy went rigid, but the man shook his head. "I'm not going to hurt you. But it's a good thing you managed to tumble Yates when you did—I didn't know where they were keeping you." He cut the ropes from Jeff's wrists. "When I take the gag off, don't bother to make a racket—it's not necessary. We're going upstairs."

A little shakily, Jeff stood up, hardly comprehending. With a grip on his arm, Morse steadied him up the stairs and out into the fresh air. When they stepped into the dancehall, the room was in such an uproar they weren't noticed for an instant. And then Harry Danver saw them and went white as china with shock and relief.

"Look—!"

The others came around in a rush. Thurston grabbed Jeff as if to make sure he was all in one piece. Pa just stood there with his hands hanging, like a man stunned.

"What happened?"

"Are you all right?"

"Stand back," ordered Morse in his cold, authorita-

224

tive way. "The boy's had a bad time of it. Get him a chair. And the rest of you sit down. I want order here!"

"Where's the Deacon?" Jeff asked weakly.

"He's gone!" one of the men exclaimed.

"Let him go." Morse shrugged. "He's only a hireling. He'll be brought to justice—I've taken precautions that he won't escape. Meanwhile— Come in, Pete."

They fell silent as the mine boss walked forward down the room. Regan looked around, his thick face reddening as he saw the hostile looks. He eyed Morse uncertainly.

"Glad you got things under control—" And then he saw Jeff. So did Sammy, who had followed Regan in. They both made an instinctive move to retreat, but Ben Thurston had stepped in behind them.

"My hands are free this time, Yates," he said readily. "No, don't touch the guns." And a couple of the miners closed in on the deputy to help relieve him of his gaudy weaponry.

"Now," Morse was going on, "I'll tell you shortly what is what here. So that you'll know I have the right to do this, I'll introduce myself. My real name is Mark Emerson."

As they stared, bewildered, Regan muttered, "I don't believe it."

"I have ample identification," the gray man told him. "And the Company's auditors will be glad to identify me. How are they making out with the account books, by the way?"

"I don't get this . . ." Pete began.

225

"You will," Morse—or Emerson—told him, with one of those frigid smiles. "What I have to say now is to these people."

Then speaking directly to the miners and their families, he went on:

"I know you're wondering what all this is about, so I'll explain. Pete Regan wrote to the head office of the Company six weeks ago and charged that the miners were getting unruly, committing sabotage. He asked my uncle to send in detectives to keep matters in hand. We happen not to like hired spies or believe in the use of force. Nor do we like the way the picture has developed in Idaho. We've seen signs, here in Montana, that our fellow companies are heading for the same trouble, but my uncle has always prided himself on being independent of these groups. He thinks enough of his own way of running a business to send me in here to look things over personally. What I've found is a thoroughly crooked manager who—"

"You can't prove a thing!" Regan barked, his face going livid.

"Oh, I think we can. At least"—Emerson smiled again—"if the auditors find one figure changed from the totals that the books showed two days ago—which I was at some pains to copy—I'll have you and your slippery friends in jail for a pleasant stay. This man who has the audacity to call himself a 'deacon' is already wanted in several states back East—he's a well-known swindler. With his help, you've been turning a neat little sum for yourself off the mine operations, I believe. And in connection with that—I have a word for our school-master."

Emerson looked over at Thurston severely. "Before you take it upon yourself to teach mining economics to your charges, better come and see me—I'll supply you with true facts. As for your theory that Company B will lose money by reason of its greed, inadequate safety, and the victimizing of its workers, it won't stand up, sir. The Bearcat has been making excellent profits under those very conditions—such profits that Mr. Regan has been able to rob the Company of sizable sums without our realizing it. Even hired his own witch doctor to keep people submissive."

"Now you listen—" Regan began again, but Emerson cut him off.

"Make your defense, if you have one, in court. The important thing now is that the mine will be reorganized under my direction for the time being, until we find a more trustworthy manager. I'm looking forward to it, as a matter of fact. It may seem curious to you, but I've come to like this town, even with all its suspicion and hostility toward me. As my stay here stretched out, I had even come to understand your mood of defiance. And then you disappointed me. You let your six leaders take the brunt of Mr. Regan's revenge without a pro-test. After that, I was unwilling to offer my proposal. I wouldn't deal with a craven lot, easily frightened out of their best intentions. I want to deal with men."

"What proposal?" ventured someone.

Emerson eyed them thoughtfully. "The Bearcat is the

property of my family. They worked for it, paid for it, and took the risks as well as the rewards," he said. "My uncle is president; his money and my grandfather's bought the land, built the tipple, and put down the shaft. They built houses for the workers, provided a store and school—I can see now they should have built churches. Someday, sole ownership of all this will descend to me. So then—does any man here think that his stake in the Bearcat is bigger than my own?"

They sat quiet and watchful.

"Do you think," he went on, "that under these circumstances I am going to let you or any other group of men tell me and my family how to run our own business? Because if that's what you have in mind, you can walk out of here now. You can strike, picket, do what you please. If you destroy our property, we'll take the same action against you that you'd take if somebody destroyed yours. It won't make any of us richer or more comfortable, but you can play it that way if you think you have the right to dictate to us."

Jeff, watching his father, saw him screw up his nerve and get to his feet. "When I'm working under loose rock, in bad air, I reckon I'm gonna feel I got *some* right to talk up."

Emerson nodded. "You'll get your timbering and ventilation—it's to nobody's advantage to have accidents, nobody's but Mr. Regan's, perhaps. Profits gained that way, at the cost of trouble with the workers, are of no long-range good. And so—my proposal. You want a union. I'm not against the idea. But it's a serious responsibility to undertake. It could become a weapon for much destruction and calamity if its rank and file are of a dispirited nature, ready to be intimidated by the first glib opportunist who may happen along. Your schoolmaster is some protection, and yet it will be a few years before his pupils are of leadership age." He glanced at Jeff.

"So," he continued, "I wasn't sure what course to take until this morning, when I stood out in back and listened to one of you stand firm against a very clever, wicked little man. Mr. Danver, I was gratified to hear you. I had hoped that you— Well, I'll have to explain that this young man of yours wrote the Company a letter, which was brought down to me by courier with some other papers a few days ago. It was an interesting letter—I was quite impressed by it. I like a son who'll stand up for his father; presumably it speaks well for the parent. In fact, your entire family has shown a good deal of stamina. That was why I came to see you the other day, intending to talk to you in my true identity. I was ready to offer you your job back on terms you could have accepted with self-respect. And then the Deacon intervened and you disappointed me. You went meekly back to a menial kind of work, against your own principles."

"That was my fault!" whispered Jeff's mother, and when she saw they had all heard her, she spoke out with surprising pluck. "I made him do it—I was scared."

"I realize that, and I sympathize," Emerson agreed. "Now today, I'm satisfied. And I say this to you, Danver: You and the men form your ranks and elect your leaders. I'll sit down with them, and I believe we'll come to terms we can all approve. I won't send a deputy, nor will I discuss your cause with anyone but your own elected representatives. I suppose the day may come when you'll feel you must join forces with some larger union—the Federation, possibly. If it does come to that, I'll regret it and I think you will, too. But I promise you that I, or one of my family, will always meet with you and respect your rights, so long as you respect ours. We won't always agree, but at least our disagreement won't be the product of confusion. That's my offer."

Danver looked around at the others. They were nodding, as hope kindled in their eyes. He turned back to Emerson and said, "Thank you, sir."

"Don't thank me. I'm not charitable. I just concur with Jefferson—a couple of Jeffersons—in the principle that the tree of liberty does exceedingly well on the blood of patriots, especially if the blood goes on coursing through our veins, where it belongs." And without the slightest trace of smile, Mark Emerson winked at Jeff.

They went home quietly. A serenity lay over the town that went a lot deeper than all that "good cheer" the Deacon had once talked of. The people hardly seemed to bear much grudge against the coachload of sullen men who had been escorted out of town, by Emerson and a small posse of miners, to be taken to the county jail.

Danver had offered to join them, but Mark had waved

him off impatiently. "Take your son home, sir," he said.

And so the family walked back down the Row together, with Pa on one side of Jeff and Ma on the other—she was crying a little, of course. The twins had been allowed to take charge of the baby; they took their responsibility so gravely that Jeff could hardly believe they were his own bobkitten sisters, until Deb managed to drift in close enough to whisper apologetically.

"When we thought you'd run away, we kind of took your marbles. But we'll give 'em back."

Jeff shook his head, trying not to laugh—he thought if he got started, he wouldn't be able to stop. Glancing over his shoulder, he caught Ben walking hand in hand with Becky. She didn't seem to mind his chin whiskers and dust. Jeff reflected that it was going to seem funny to have to say "Mister" to his best friend and brother-in-law. And yet, anything else would hardly be proper for a schoolroom.

He hoped Pa was going to understand about that and not be irked if he even maybe went on through high school. Anxiously, he glanced up at his father.

Harry Danver was watching him with a curious side-long look that was almost shy. For a minute, they were like two strangers, strangers who pretty well liked each other. Then Pa grinned, clamped a strong arm across his son's shoulders—and Jeff didn't worry any more.